PRAISE FOR
BENJAMIN TAYLOR'S
TALES OUT OF SCHOOL

Winner of the Harold Ribalow Prize

"A beautifully rendered, moving, original debut. . . . Taylor writes in a richly poetic language steeped in time and place, a powerful style that well supports the tale of the Mehmel family. . . . His magical, expressive language pulls the [story] rapidly along."
—*Kirkus Reviews* (starred review)

"[A] powerful first novel. . . . Taylor's spare, supple prose easily accommodates effective forays into magic realism as well as nuanced evocations of the desire, religious doubt, and affection that animate his memorable characters."
—*Publishers Weekly* (starred review)

"All the great themes . . . sibling rivalry, generational conflict, birth, death, and the magical, miserable phenomenon of love. . . . The beauty of Taylor's language—ratchets up and down from lyrical exposition to hardscrabble dialogue. His elaborate idiom allows him to sound certain metaphysical depths, to explore what he calls 'this abyss of humanness into which we reach, not knowing where the bottom lies.'"
—JAMES MARCUS, *Newsday*

SELECTED AS ONE OF
GAY CHICAGO MAGAZINE'S
10 BEST NOVELS OF 1995

more . . .

"This is a story of melancholy and regret, of loss and mostly resignation, a story that interweaves a bizarre cast of characters that somehow drift onto the island and stick. . . . Mr. Taylor has written a novel that . . . flows and swells with powerful language."
—*Dallas Morning News*

"The writing is splendid, the story absorbing and wrenching. . . . An astonishing debut."
—LYNNE SHARON SCHWARTZ

"Some prose invites being heard. . . . Benjamin Taylor's language is lush, exotic, at times peculiar, as befits a novel set on Galveston Island, Texas, where the extraordinary finds a fertile environment at the beginning of this century. Catholic, Jew, redneck, homosexual—these mix, marry, exchange vocabularies and dialects. Latin and Hebrew are sung on the Texas shore. It's a setting where Taylor feels confident to fit rare words to a rare locale."
—*Riverfront Times* (St. Louis)

"TALES OUT OF SCHOOL reads like a haunting and significant dream, the key to a previous life."
—LILY TUCK

"A magical and mysterious work."
—EDWARD ALBEE

"A lyrical evocation of time recaptured . . . [and] of stories interconnected and so hauntingly told that we are hypnotized by the sheer force of Taylor's style. I have not read paragraphs this good, this informed about history . . . for quite some time."
—SANFORD PINSKER,
Philadelphia Jewish Exponent

"A tale of the Tribe as enmeshed with harebrained circumstance as it is with heretical myth. Classical resonance, I learn from reading this affectionate affabulation, has nothing to do with grand scale, it is the grand style that works the mystery—and the mischief. What a lovable, brilliant recital!"
—RICHARD HOWARD

"I enjoyed the book immensely; it is a wonderfully beguiling vision."
—AMITAV GHOSH

"The novel is about other days and other people: their eccentricities and interdependences. But the wonder of this book is its style. Through that, it is made to be a story that draws the reader into an enchanting moment and holds the attention from sentence to sentence. Ben Taylor's real achievement is to restore the tension and magic of song to narrative."
—EAVAN BOLAND

"I didn't want the book to end, and its long reverie stays with me."
—RACHEL HADAS

"Dryly humorous and moving, learned and colloquial, lyrical and richly suggestive. . . . Taylor's vision is an idealistic one, but it is none the less effective."
— *Times Literary Supplement* (London)

"One of the great novels of the decade. If you have to, steal a copy."
— *Gay Times* (London)

ALSO BY BENJAMIN TAYLOR

Into the Open: Reflections on Genius and Modernity

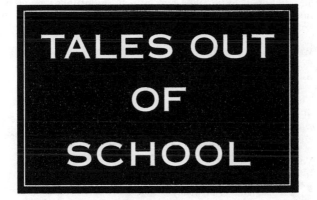

TALES OUT OF OF SCHOOL

BENJAMIN TAYLOR

WARNER BOOKS

A Time Warner Company

Warner Books Edition
Copyright © 1995 by Benjamin Taylor
All rights reserved.

This Warner Books edition is published by arrangement with Turtle Point Press, New York, NY

Warner Books, Inc., 1271 Avenue of the Americas, New York, NY 10020

Visit our Web site at
http://pathfinder.com/twep

W A Time Warner Company

Printed in the United States of America
First Warner Books Printing: April 1997
10 9 8 7 6 5 4 3 2 1

Library of Congress Cataloging-in-Publication Data

Taylor, Benjamin
      Tales out of school / Benjamin Taylor.
          p. cm.
      ISBN 0-446-67269-6
      I. Title.
      [PS3570.A92714T35 1997]
      813'.54—dc20   96-9641
                                                              CIP

Cover design by Cynthia Krupat
Cover art: Detail from "Youth" c. 1882-84 by Helene Schjerfbeck

To Amy and Pete, beloved ones.

Contents

Tales Out of School

CHAPTER ONE

Galveston Island, 1907

T HAT WAS THE HOUSE where the Jews lived. Manifesting his means, Aharon Mehmel had caused it to be built of limestone and blue granite, roofed with green tiles, bordered by high wrought iron. Oleander grew there; also fig and orange and palm. From third-floor dormers along the southern side, you looked clean out to sea.

In the vestibule, fastening on a picture hat, turning her back to the mirror for another look at the flounced skirt drawn into a bustle, stood Lucy Pumphrey Mehmel, seven years a widow—or "relic" of Aharon Mehmel as hereabouts they said.

Tales Out of School

Today, June third, was Decoration Day, signified by veterans parading up the Strand, flowers on graves of the Confederate dead, and at the Customs House a lunch of roast chicken, steamed cabbage, and blancmange for dessert. Dressed in the style of the year before last, Lucy made her way to town. People when they saw her smiled remotely, and squared their shoulders as they said, "Good day," and gave each other knowing glances when the widow Mehmel had passed by. The last couple of years in particular had done for her, people said. A gentlewoman with a hidden vice, people said. And a drawerful of duns, people said. And an abyss in her. Gaiety and melancholia alternating. Some days she would dress up fine; some days she would not leave her darkened room.

So as to avoid passing by this residence or that shop, the widow Mehmel nowadays took long cuts to town, her path growing ever more circuitous. And this morning what she saw was that no meander was left, that all routes had become impassable. She turned around; she went back home.

On Lucy's doorpost you found the customary

parchment, affixed in a copper case, inscribed with sacred words and a sacred name, declaring the Lord God to be One God. But from a chain around her neck, secreted in a locket, for no one but herself to know about, hung Christ on the Cross, saving humankind.

Here she was in the late September of her beauty, still with that head of raffia hair that had always been the talk. Here she was in her late September. Being beautiful had been—interesting. Now there was time enough to wonder what the other life would have been. Say, that of Molly, her sister, obese and with a riot of pimples on her. These two girls, God help the latter, had been referred to as "the twins." It wasn't meant as cruel. Who could have foreseen what a plainness Molly'd turn out to be? Born more than seven months apart, they were certainly and definitely not twins. Here is the truth: Lucy was Mr. Pumphrey's by his duly wedded wife, but Molly by a shadowy mistress who had abandoned her spawn to the Pumphrey front step. By way of explanation a not at all fulsome note was attached to one little wrist: *This rug rat's yours, Pum-*

phrey, was all it said, and it was aplombly signed by Miss Lurlena Grovner, who'd had all she could bear of shame and was going to Chicago.

Lucy was now thirty-three years of age and had not laid eyes on her supposititious twin since the two of them were eighteen. Not that they'd lost touch. Back and forth the letters flew between New Orleans and Galveston Island.

"How can you stand that little bit of a place he took you to?" Molly at the outset inquired.

"Here's home to me," came the answer. "I don't miss your New Orleans one bit."

Lucy had made modest inroads into the German language, Aharon tutoring in the dark, persuading from her now and again some whispered indecency not to be said in her own tongue. Afterwards, talking long and late, she'd find she could not say, in any language, the tithe of what she had to say, love so utter it seemed a privation to close her eyes for sleep.

At the start of their second year of marriage, a most important letter to Molly: "Tell Mama she's a grandmother, as of two days ago. Yes, a little boy, name of Felix. Do you think that's a good name?

Galveston Island, 1907

If Aharon doesn't stop me, I am going to eat this child with a spoon!" Molly for her part did not fail to keep Lucy posted. After four years of marking time, "I'm married, sister!" was the great good news. A fine man, a hard worker—oh, maybe a little older than one would have wished, certainly no Croesus, no more for all markets than the radiant bride herself, but a *man* and this was the point.

Seasons came and went; letters too. "Luce, I don't feel myself unless I'm in the family way." This had turned out to be the one string to Molly's harp. "I reckon I'll just go on having more and more. How many babies can a woman have? They say there's a Cajun gal in Bogalusa who's got the record at twenty-six. I like to threw a jealous fit when I heard about it. So may I ask what's a matter with you with only your one? Do you want people to call you selfish? Because that's what you're being. Yes, selfish not to have a brood!"

Lucy did not respond to any of this exhortation, which slopped over from letter to letter. There was no question of telling Molly the truth, and Lucy hadn't the stomach for a lie. What had befallen was a thing not politely talked about, and even if she'd been minded to speak of it she would not have known how. Turning the tremendous word over in her mind, she noticed that when repeated again and again it got loose of what it stood for, became just as nice a bunch of syllables as mignonette, or coquelicot, or girandole. Yes, a pretty word, syphilis, if you could but disregard what it meant.

Aharon had it.

He'd gone to Houston on business. A very promising parcel of fifty acres was to be auctioned off in a bankruptcy there and Gerson Mehmel, founder and president of the Sweet Brook Brewery, had sent his elder boy, his good right hand, his able Aharon, the one of two sons with a head for getting rather than just spending money, to have a look see. Yonder land was a fine black humus earth, right for growing hops, not poor and salt and sandy as in Galveston. It might be an excellent investment for them. Aharon determined that it was and bid successfully for it. Wiring the news back to his father, he included a message of dearest love to Lucy and to their six-month-old little boy. "With you posthaste—Aharon."

Galveston Island, 1907

Why do men do the things they do? Why don't they do better? A second telegram said: "Arranging title. Detained until Monday." Then came a third: "With you by Friday." Then a fourth, announcing "unforeseen difficulties." It was near two weeks later that Aharon finally did turn up, the worse for wear. When Lucy tried to kiss him he put his hand between her lips and his. This frightened her considerably. She implored what the matter was. She followed him upstairs and to their room. More of his silence. He began opening and shutting drawers, gathering up belongings—toiletries, shirts, some underclothes—and was carrying them to the spare room at the other end of the hall when she came on from behind, eyes flashing, and knocked it all from his hands. "You talk to me, Aharon Mehmel! You *talk* to me!"

He bent down to pick up the starched folded shirts, the shaving mug and brush, the bar of soap. He looked up with a stricken smile. "Doctor says."

"Doctor who? Says what?"

"Doctor in Houston, says I'm sick. A very mild case. Says it's a little catching though. Through the skin. But very mild. Says I'll be better off sleeping by myself, for now."

A little catching, through the skin. Never once had he taken her for an idiot until this moment. "Aharon, what are you saying?" She'd heard sufficient stories about his younger days to make the inference from then to now. It had been her prospective mother-in-law, that disobliging, strange-natured woman, who took her aside one evening for an earful about the various muslins young Aharon had got himself tangled up in. Mostly girls from the north side of the Island, she said, where the poor and near-poor reside. But one or two from the quality too. Liselotte Mehmel said the boy she'd raised was no different from any other; said they all think a homely piece of sheep's bowel hanging between the legs makes gods of them.

She warned the little bride-to-be about males of the species, how they lodge their manhood harum-scarum where they may. Now Aharon had the chancre, raspberry bold, in evidence. This has arisen "at the site of inoculation" (doctor's way of putting the matter) about five days following his casualness, enlarged rapidly, then broke open at the centre, leaving a shallow ulcer. Doctor in Houston took one look and knew.

Aharon on the floor amid his belongings had begun to cry: "I'd sooner die—*die!*—than pass this to you!" She wondered for an instant, a life instant, what next thing she would do. Tear the skin from his head and neck? Break his lost-to-shame body with her hands?

Neither. She sat down on the floor with him. Was there a name for the emotion that beat upon her? It wasn't hatred, or anger; either of these would have been convenient. It wasn't forgiveness. Lucy pulled a handkerchief from her sleeve and handed it to Aharon. It surely wasn't desire . . . It was love that comes after love, after the expulsion from inexperience.

"Can you get well? People sometimes get well, don't they?"

"Doctor says the treatments are all like having another disease—and they don't any of them work either. He says there's somebody in Hamburg who's going to find something—someday, maybe soon. I've got his name and address right here. I'm going to write him a letter."

Tales Out of School

There are choices you make not by planning but (as you make your shadow) by being where you are. Where you are and not somewhere else. Seeing her husband, his gaze inward-turned as that of an animal in a trap, Lucy chose him, chose him all over again for her own. She considered putting her arms around his shaking shoulders, but didn't. She just kept her seat on the floor beside him.

Syphilis goes forward in stages. After three or four weeks the chancre heals, leaving no scar, and thus the first stage ends. Next comes an interregnum or honeymoon, tempting the patient to believe himself in good case. But after the interregnum, the onset of stage two with its patchy loss of hair; coppery-red papules appearing even on the palms and soles; mucosal ulcers besetting the mouth, the eyes, the anus. These secondary symptoms subside within a few months. And then comes the long, long cakewalk of seeming health—years or even decades of it. Then, at last, the tertiary stage, and here the great pretender does what he wants with you: turns your spinal column to glass or your aorta to stone, strikes your eyes with blindness, scrambles your reason. He is not to be evaded.

Aharon did his best several times to write that letter to the esteemed Herr Doktor So-and-So of Hamburg, but discovered that he could not put the right words together in German. It had been the medium of his upbringing, spoken with pleasure and precision by his parents and imparted to their sons as a thing to be reverenced—the language of Goethe and Schiller, the language of Heine!

Gerson and Liselotte Mehmel had brought their Europe with them to America. She played pianoforte; he, the violoncello. Aharon played viola, and gloriously. Leo, their younger boy, did what he could on violin. Several nights a week they sat down to *Hausmusik*: piano quartets of Mozart, Hummel, Weber, Spohr, Mendelssohn-Bartholdy—particularly the slow movements, which Leo could negotiate, though just. (Scherzos and allegros were another matter.) Sometimes Papa would suggest that Leo hand over the violin to his big brother. "Listening is as fine an art as playing, son." And if he was balky Mama would point a finger and say,

"*Liebling*, we are going to play trios now. Give your brother the violin." Then Papa and Mama and Aharon would launch into (say) the great Haydn trio in F-sharp minor or the Beethoven "Archduke" or the Opus 8 of Brahms. Leo would dash from Mama to Papa to Aharon, obligingly turning pages, and Papa would permit himself to look up and smile confidentially at his younger boy, his Leo to whom things did not come easily.

Best of all, according to Leo, was when Mama and Papa played duos—typically one or the other of the Mendelssohn cello sonatas, the B-flat or the D-flat, and these in the long aftertime had come to embody intimacy and swift sureness for him. Also a mocking remoteness.

There were other evenings Papa would take down a masterpiece from the hoard of German literature and read aloud. Every blessed word of *Wilhelm Meister* over the course of an autumn and a winter. Novels of Tieck and Jean Paul and Keller and Eichendorf and Stifter. No end of these literary holdings forth, by which Gerson Mehmel sought to compensate his sons—for having taken them from a real civilization, for having carried them across wide water to this America, this expedient, this last recourse, good for making money, that was all.

And indeed, like sparks from a flint, Gerson Mehmel had struck his fortune from the new land. When they arrived he took a taste of the pond water that passed locally for beer and said: "We can do better." The trouble, he believed, was owing to a too-hasty malting process, the barley kilned without allowing adequate time for germination. There is no making good beer from a bad malt. No corn or rice in the mashing, no care in the filtration of the wort, no flavoring with hop blossom, no length of ageing will yield a good product if the barley you start with has been improperly sprouted. This unimpeachable first axiom of brewing became the credo of Gerson Mehmel. What Galveston Island needed was a good pilsner, he felt, pale amber as the usual lager but more strongly flavored. After considerable misses he struck finally on the right preparations, the right boiling times, the right vessels in which to ferment and to age. Having brought about through trial and error something new under the sun, he packed a bottle of it in shaved ice and went to ask Mr. Lyman Smalley, president of the First Trust of Galveston, would he like a taste? "Don't mind if I do," said Mr. Smalley, who took a slow draught, sat forward in his chair: "Delicious, Mehmel, absolutely delicious!"

Banker Smalley wondered with pleasure was this the promised end, had earth quit its fixed course to swing out on paths unknown when he, a Christian, hastened to lend out money at interest to Mehmel, a Jew?

"How much will you be needing, Mehmel?"

Smalley was a bald man who wore a straw boater in the summer months and, under the boater, a dampened washcloth. The boater he hung on his office door, the washcloth he kept on his head. "Fifteen hundred, you say? Well, fifteen hundred is a considerable sum, young man." He went on like this, giving Mehmel the business. He liked him that well. "Would you not agree with me that fifteen hundred is a considerable sum? Quite out of the question, I'm bound to say." But Smalley had seen the angel of luck dance this way and that behind Mehmel.

One thousand five hundred dollars, at one and five eighths per cent. Done.

In six years Mehmel turned this fifteen hundred into a hundred thousand. In another six he conjured that into more than a quarter of a million. After yet another six, his beard and temples silvered through, his sons leafing out into manhood, Gerson Mehmel had learned to comport himself with all serenity behoving Galveston's sixth richest citizen. Or was it fifth? Or fourth? Among a provincial gentry there were compelling reasons to know from year to year exactly who stood where.

Mehmel stood increasingly to the fore. Certain ones, to be sure, murmured about his brilliant rise. How did it happen that he unfailingly anticipated trends? He had a nearly diabolical gift for staying ahead of the business cycles, reaping his profit, it was claimed, in the lean times as well as the fat. What dowsing wand did he employ? the harmlessly jealous wondered. But there were a darkling harmful few who theorized that Mehmel not only benefited from but provoked these economic ups and downs, that the vaunted invisible hand of the market was in reality his.

"Oh, that clever German," the harmless declared.

Replied the harmful, "He's not a German but a Jew."

Not that they were unwilling, the harmless and not harmless alike, to attend a musical evening at Mehmel's house if invited. These were very satisfactory occasions, with guest performers from out of town and claret cup afterwards. No great audience could be accommodated at one time, however; the Mehmels still resided in the modest carpenter Gothic at Sealy and Sixteenth that had been their dwelling for twenty years. With its shiplap and lattice painted white and shutters and flower boxes picked out in deep green, it was certainly a pretty house, though with nothing magniloquent about it, nothing to tell of the rise of Mehmel. And while he naturally did think now and then of removing with his family to one of the baronial places along Broadway, Liselotte firmly rejected the idea each time it was put forth.

"Bottom of the top drawer is the place for us," she would declare, ending further discussion.

The steadfast link binding Lucy Pumphrey Mehmel's womanhood to her girlhood, binding Galveston to New Orleans—that had been old Neevah Sharoard. Accompanied by her, Lucy and Molly Pumphrey arrived in the summer of 1891 for a visit of two weeks to family friends. Sixteen years later, here Lucy and Neevah still were.

Being one place or the other was no matter to Neevah Sharoard. In her view most of life was pure child foolishness, a truth as true wherever you stayed so where you stayed made no difference. Neevah maintained with ferocious laughter that the real life is the one to come and that we are like passengers on a drawn-out sea voyage, most of us unable even to recollect where it is we're going. But amid this confusion and sorrow, somebody catches the scent of land. "Right under your noses, churren." She was the colored woman, freed at age

Tales Out of School

thirty-two, seventy-six now, who had slept beside Lucy and Molly until they were eighteen.

Neevah had once had a husband, but now could remember him only in the vague. *That* kind of love had never in her long life tempted again, for reasons she invoked happily about. First the blast of hilarity, then the pearl of wisdom. "Lucy, Molly, mens is *bad!*" She would laugh and be right in her laughter; but neither laughter nor cajolery nor anything had availed sixteen years previous when, following their graduation from the Convent School of the Ursulines, she accompanied the two Miss Pumphreys, along with their pair of Brussels gryphons, for an August visit to Galveston. Lucy was edgy, excitable, bucking for her release. Poor Neevah's commission was to keep the girl intact.

"How do. I'm Lucy Pumphrey—from Newawlens?" On the boat she had said this to a total stranger, handsome and as it turned out a bachelor. Neevah shook her head, shook till her hat was like to come off. When the ship's bell rang for five the Miss Pumphreys went below to dress. "That one," Lucy said to Molly.

· 18 ·

"But Luce, you don't know a blessed thing about him."

"*That* one."

Oh, there were the familiar likely fellows back in New Orleans—a dim-wit jaundiced bunch whose folderol Lucy had listened to for long enough. "I'm going to meet myself a *smart* man!" she'd hollered one night, rounding angrily on their mother, poor thing, who'd waited up to ask, "Nice party, dears?" when Lucy and Molly got home from the Saint Alphonsus Sociable Ball . . .

A noon meal of crawfish étouffée and root beer was being served next noon on the upper deck of the steamer. "Miss Pumphrey, will you and your sister join me for lunch?" Thus the note awaiting Lucy when she waked up. "Delighted, Mr. Mehmel" was the reply she hastened back. Poor Neevah, who had not lived to be sixty-one for nothing, could scc that events were getting ahead of her. Of course, the girls were always thoroughly chaperoned in New Orleans, as they would be during their Galveston stay. Only for this brief passage across the Gulf were they in Neevah's uncertain charge.

This Mr. Mehmel had violet eyes: smoky, unfamiliar. And a smile like a flock of sheep coming at you, which he plentifully flashed when the two young ladies ascended to the fore deck, their Brussels gryphons, Jaloux and Jalouse, heeling beside them.

Neevah, meantime, brooded in steerage.

At lunch young Aharon abstained from the étouffée, claiming not to be hungry, but drank glass after glass of root beer, toasting Galveston in it, and New Orleans, and most of all the Miss Pumphreys.

"Étouffée is dee-vine," Molly affirmed through a mouthful of it. "Mr. Mehmel, you got to have some. Pass him some, Luce." This urging went on until Aharon quietly allowed as he ate only those aquatic animals which had fins and scales and did not bottom feed. Molly said, "Mr. Mehmel, those are the silliest cry-teer-i-als I ever heard," and decided there and then she did not like him. Jaloux and Jalouse were behaving beautifully, and Molly commenced to say so. "Sweet girl! Fine boy!" They inclined their ears to her, then grew weary. Jaded looks passed between them. "We think they deserve a nice walk on the lower deck, Molly," said Lucy with the minimum of emphasis. To starboard the spindrift was breaking up into vermilion and gold and, lo, the very violet of Aharon Mehmel's gaze. Under his eyes, Lucy saw, were bluish shadows, a past and future written there . . .

Now, sixteen years later, she marveled at the unlikeliness. None of this was as her life was supposed to be. There had been with Aharon a new conjugal language to learn, an old one to try to forget. His body had, at first, repelled her when she learned what it harbored. She imagined beneath the well-knit flesh—vermoulure, corruption, living death. Aharon was accountably timid and undemanding in his new state, and for months they remained thus at a standstill, she revolted and he ashamed. Hours together some nights he would stand at her bedroom door. Then, silent on sock feet, he at last began to steal in. He would watch her sleep awhile, then hasten away. This went on for some nights, over the course of which Aharon got braver, kneeling close enough to get a feel of Lucy's unpinned hair.

Trembling there one night before her, like a

youth with no first notion, Aharon unbuttoned his shirt and pants. Lucy stirred then, wakened perhaps by the shadow of a moonlit hand reaching out for her, or by the catch in Aharon's breath, or by the close prevalent odor of him. There came to her a sudden hectic recollection of other times. Such was its vehemence that the past seemed to become the future.

"We must be careful," Aharon whispered, "absolutely careful." No, past could not become future. That route was stopped up by angels and a flashing sword. What was given them now to invent was the sad new ceremonies of love: vigilant, guarded, permitting of no return to the old ways.

Aharon feared disgrace, as it turned out, more than the disease itself. He and Lucy took every precaution to keep the truth from circulating. "Ruined lives, ruined lives"—were it known, that is what people would say; and turn to go about their business. It is unendurable, even if the way of the world, that one's fate should turn resistlessly into chitchat of others.

Ruined lives.

Galveston Island, 1907

The one to find out was Dr. Bidwell, Aharon's physician, to whom he went with recurring back pain from an old injury, a strained sacroiliac. Dr. Bidwell, a square-jawed Yankee sort without words to spare, asked the patient to disrobe and performed his examination.

A lengthy silence.

"Mr. Mehmel, you are aware of these lesions on your arms and back? On the evidence of these, I believe you may have syphilis."

Bidwell made a notation in Aharon's chart, underscored it twice, reiterated the warnings about private conduct Aharon had heard in Houston.

"You may rely on my discretion, Mr. Mehmel. I only ask that you make a point of seeing me at least once a month. And your wife, has she, forgive my having to ask, has she been—examined, for symptoms?"

Aharon raised a forfending arm, let it drop, shook his head. "I was away, in Houston, when I got sick."

"You are certain there has been no occasion for the disease, forgive me, to pass from you to her?"

"Absolutely," said Aharon, his voice rising.

But Dr. Bidwell went on equably: "Be grateful that you and she are blessed with at least one child. There can be no question of another, as I'm sure you understand. You must allow yourself no delusions, Mr. Mehmel. For Mrs. Mehmel's sake. For the sake of the child you and she might conceive."

Ruined lives. From time to time Liselotte Mehmel would stare measuringly at her elder son, as if she knew backwards and forwards the whole wretched truth; but then start in on light by-the-way conversational matters, and shift her eyes askance. What was she thinking? Who knew?

The elder Mehmels had habits of longstanding which it was unthinkable to infringe. For instance, their evening constitutional. Every night, weather permitting, they would take an after-supper stroll through the neighborhood. As Aharon and Lucy then lived only six doors downstreet on Avenue J, it was not unlikely at eight or nine o'clock to have the folks turn up seeking for postprandial coffee and conversation.

They had a way of knocking symbolically as they

strode in. One night, not long after Aharon's trip to Houston, the elder Mehmels found Aharon at the dining-room table poring over a large architectural plan. He had weighted the corners of it with encyclopaedia volumes; he had pulled over a floor lamp which pooled brightly down onto the blueprint. And what was that on the sideboard? A handsome scale model submitted by Messrs. Barnett, Haynes & Barnett—renowned architectural firm to the nabobs and magnificoes of far-off splendid Saint Louis, Missouri—along with their proposal. Lucy had been opening and shutting the windows and doors of the little house. It had removable storeys. She'd taken off the roof in order to examine the third floor; then the third floor to examine the second; then, finally, the second for a look at the first with its circular foyer, double-length drawing room, galleries front and back. Lucy's fingers ambled in and out of the many rooms, up and down the curving flights of stairs. And nowhere to be found was what chance—who is no architect—had added: the ruin cutting a hard swath through.

Roused from her bemusement, there she found them. It would have been as well if the elder Mehmels had not turned up just then. Aharon was waiting for an opportune time to present his and Lucy's undertaking, which he knew his mother would not like. Having plans thus spread out at this hour of the evening was a risk he and Lucy had unwisely run.

Aharon looked scared. But Lucy, resolute. She would, by God, see built what the blueprint depicted. Iron had entered her along with the sorrow. She would have the fine Broadway plot of land, four blocks north and two west of where they currently lived. She would see rise there the splendid limestone and blue granite edifice with its three storeys and screened sleeping porches and graceful curving stair.

Of necessity, a family scene ensued, Aharon pleading for the down payment out of brewery profits, Liselotte swearing he would get it over her dead person, Gerson in anguish trying to make the peace. As for Lucy, she knew these differences would be settled—albeit with much inventive carrying on—in her and Aharon's favor and therefore said nothing, held aloof from the fray.

Rubbing his chin, a signal of distress, Papa invoked the ethos of saving rather than spending. Mama leapt in to declare that the business would find itself undercapitalized if such sums were siphoned away—"for a folly," as she put it. She said fancy mansions are where you live before you betake yourself to the poorhouse.

Lucy didn't pay either of her in-laws any attention that night. The quarrel between Aharon and his parents was local, after all. Whereas Lucy had discovered the infinite. The infinite of her objection. Her objection to what had happened. She would make of her objection a great stone house.

Next morning, having stayed up late to wrest an assurance from his parents, who passed from anger to entreaties to bafflement, Aharon set off to the First Trust of Galveston to speak with Chairman of the Board Lyman Smalley.

The years by now had scaled Smalley down. He sat precariously forward in a tufted leather chair, his white shoes no longer to the floor, delivering the awful "no" or sought-for "yes" in a high batlike whisper. Clerks leaned close to hear the verdict, then hastened to an adjoining room to communicate it to the loan applicant in regretful or congratulatory tones, depending. This was customary, but Aharon had insisted on a private audience with the Chairman of the Board in order to make his case.

Diminished though he now was in mind as in body, Smalley recognized the young man standing before him, hat in hand. He studied Aharon, then studied his financial statement. Liverishly, he shook his head. It wasn't anything in the documents, for these bespoke the finest prospects. It was that through a failing eye he'd plainly seen the angel of luck—who ought to have danced—turn on her rugged heel. Through the wainscot she was gone.

Smalley's young assistants had a way of passing confidential looks over their employer's head. They considered that he should retire. Smalley said to Aharon that two or three years earlier, when the economy had troughed, would have been more opportune. He said that the current year, 1892, had been one of notable uptrends; that 1893 promised further growth. He pointed out to Aharon that he'd be building at the top of the market, paying dear for land, materials, labor.

"Unseasonable, young man."

But did these dissuasions make any sense from the bank's point of view? Decidedly not. Young Mehmel was a very sound opportunity for them. Again the clerks gave each other looks. Would Smalley like to lose this loan, was that it?

Ah, these popinjays did not hear what the Chairman of the Board had heard—chalky rustle of wings in the wallspace, seraphic mutters.

Aharon was feeling desperate, had all but folded his hands to beg. But presently behind him through the wainscot stepped a different angel, a dark one. Smalley saw and was frightened. Smalley spent no more words, only signed in sorrow the mortgage instrument and showed Aharon the place where he too should sign.

CHAPTER TWO

Empty Hands

THE ELDER MEHMELS' HOUSE at Sealy and Sixteenth was furnished with but one extravagance, a front door of fretted cypress wood. It was Gerson Mehmel's particular pride. Cypress will not rot, he had explained to his two sons when they were young. He took a deep comfort from the fact, would in watches of the night go down to the front hall and swing the door back and forth on its polished hinges, saying, "Cypress will not rot," spilling his words onto the night air. That was before.

Or he would take Aharon and Leo up to the attic and show them a hundred-pound bag of lentils

kept there. "My sons, we could live on lentils if we had to." That, too, was before.

Now was after. Now Lucy came to call each day on a Gerson Mehmel who was not his former strength. "*Schöne Dame*," he would say when she came silently through the bedroom door, and point to a spot on his cheek where she should kiss him.

"Mama said you might be sleeping, she didn't know."

Whether he was chilled or just shaking with his infirmity, she could not tell. She opened the settle, drew from it a purple Indian blanket with diamonds and eagles alternating, covered her father-in-law up to the neck, tucked the border close around him. His mottled hands traced yellow and green shapes against the purple ground. "*Hübsch*," he said.

"Aharon brought it to you, Papa, remember?" His son had brought it home twelve years before, from the City of Mexico. Drawing the linseed-smelling robe from its wrappings, Aharon had said, with a grin, "For your old age, Papa." And so it was. And soon.

They had all been in synagogue when the Great

Storm came on. The Sabbath dawn of September 8th, 1900, showed a sky like brick dust, always a portent hereabouts. By nine-thirty, when the Mehmels arrived for their worship, the air was turning to mother-of-pearl, radiantly pink and yet refracting all the rainbow colors in a fish-scale effect. By eleven, when the Scroll of the Law was taken down for reading, a high wind had begun to yammer. Aharon told his people to stay, he would go to the brewery and secure what he could, then come back.

Outside, water rushed axle-high up Sealy Street. The Gulf had risen five or six feet in only an hour. Gale winds flattened the surface; underneath ran a vicious undertow. First of the many dreadful things Aharon saw was a woman and two children whipsawed off their feet. Little legs and arms flashed briefly in the scud. The woman surfaced, mouth agape, hands flailing water.

In the wind were many voices. An old man brokenly prayed. A boy keened for his mother. A woman hugging a piece of drift shouted that this was not weather but the end of the world.

Still caught in the traces, a pair of walleyed

horses thrashed by. Slate tiles flew through the air. Also timbers, tin sheathing, two-by-fours, creosoted paving blocks, shingles, lath. A hellish rainfall had commenced. Gulf waters and harbor waters were closing over Galveston. Aharon watched Adelson's Dry Goods at Twenty-eighth and Ball Street rise off its piers, majestic, like a great steamboat. And watched the smaller structures, torn apart like blotting paper. He bellied himself onto a doorfacing which floated past. Current and wind, he saw through the rainspray, were driving everything before them, living and dead together, into a fused mass of wreckage.

What did he feel? Shame for his life.

Along came an uprooted cottonwood, flayed of its leaves, tossed like a shuttlecock in the crosscurrents. And seated astride of it was old Mr. Orvis Truley, the town madman. When he caught sight of Aharon he gave a chipper smile and a nautical wave.

Poor Orvis, too damned crazy to be scared. Beholding him, as if by some mystery of impartation, Aharon shed his own fear. He leapt for the cottonwood, in the upper branches of which was a tangled length of rope. Aharon's purpose now was to tie down Orvis, who wouldn't last long just blithely sitting there without even a notion of danger to his credit.

But to tie down Orvis was not easy, for this was a large unruly man. When Aharon looped the rope around him Orvis began to struggle with all his animal strength, years' worth of it he'd pent up, for a fit of sanity had now come over him. Fits of sanity often did. Popular opinion notwithstanding, Orvis wasn't really mad at all, Orvis was *angry* and had learned to cloak anger in a convenient lunacy. Now the cloak fell away. He could abide all manner of abuse but not this, not to be tied to a tree. Orvis bared his rotten teeth at Aharon as if to bite him. He hissed as Aharon made the rope fast.

Mehmel was, in his own mind, but seeing to a needful task. He didn't thus mean to spend the last of himself, didn't mean to offer up his life for the town madman. But suddenly, along with the presence of those left behind—mother, father, wife, child—there came utter heaviness, as if lead were coursing through him. A blaze in the marrow, then

letting go, the beckoning of night and surcease,
against which love makes its case . . .

Mother, father, wife, child . . .

The beckoning of night and surcease, against
which love makes its slender case . . .

Orvis reached out, managing to save no more of
Aharon Mehmel than the Sabbath shirt off his
back.

Along the somewhat higher ridge of ground that
was Broadway, where manufacturers and shippers
and merchants outvied each other in magnitude
and solidity and lavishness—Silk Shirt Boulevard,
people called it—the flood waters had not reached
to second-storey rooms. It was more than strange
when tides receded next day, Sunday, to find the
downstairs of your house deprived of everything
water could compel through windows or doors
(even the Bechstein was somehow gone) and yet
discover a book in the upstairs sitting room still
face down at the page where you had left off reading Friday night; or, beside your bed, just as
you arranged them, cinnamon roses you had on
Thursday gone down to the arbor to cut . . .

Now bluebottles swarmed behind a drayload of dead coming past. Smells of carbolic, lime, putrefaction were in the air. Mayor Hoak Tilden, having placed Galveston under martial law, directed that the thousands of dead be buried quickly, at sea, without exception. He conscripted laborers to pile the unspeakable cargo onto barges, doling out bourbon to blunt the men's revulsion, impressing at gunpoint any who shied from the task.

At about three o'clock that Sunday afternoon, having entrusted little Felix to Neevah's care, Lucy Mehmel arranged a shawl so as to cover her head and the lower half of her face and made her way down to what survived of the dockyards. Either she did not hear or else paid no mind to deputies clenching cigars in their teeth who urged her back from a wharf where the dead in windrows lay. She managed to lift one or two of the tarpaulins and would have methodically made her way up and down the shrouded ranks had she not been forcibly restrained.

"Have to ask you to leave, ma'am."

"I'm looking for my husband," Lucy uncovered

her face long enough to say, then hurriedly replaced the shawl. "I'm looking for my husband," she said again, muffled this time.

Aharon had walked every weekday morning from the great stone house on Broadway, since its recent completion, to the modest shiplap house at Sealy and Sixteenth in order to collect his father for the brewery office. Now it was his widow Lucy who came calling—in order to see a father-in-law irretrievably ill.

After the hurricane Gerson Mehmel had grieved wildly for his elder son, turning more and more feral in his habits, refusing to wash or shave or cut the hair he would draw back with dirty talons, unshrouding the blank of his gaze. He rejected all civilities of home, consuming only bread and beer, emptying his bowels and bladder where he pleased out of doors, bedding down in the spidery cellardamp. Imaginary noises beset him: by night, the churning of the stars and planets; by day, the jeering bellow of God. His old violoncello—a genuine Amati—he shrank from now in confoundment.

There were spells, infrequent but sufficiently terrible, in which Mr. Mehmel believed his gone-missing son to have come home, salt and gulf mire clinging to him still. Liselotte could think of nothing on these occasions but to sit down to the piano, tears marking her face, and play something *forte* while her brainsick husband doted and raved.

It was said that a lesser woman would be broken by such griefs as Mrs. Mehmel bore. There was her Gerson who sat glaring by the hour into his empty hands. And that awfully nice elder son who had died heroical in the Storm. And that wretched surviving son, the younger one, who'd never done a day's work in his life, behaved more like a woman than a man, and was the family disgrace. God love her, everybody said, even those she took to task. Retailed lately with satisfaction was how on the trolley-bus a fractious youth had blocked her way and how Liselotte Mehmel, pronouncing several aspersions, had struck him in the face with her steel-beaded reticule. Far from diminishing Mrs. Mehmel in Galveston's eyes, occasions such as this were cherished; her temper had become a trust of the place and source of civic pride.

CHAPTER THREE

Walnuts,
When the Husks Are Green

REE-WHEELING UP THE DRIVE on his bicycle, arms across his chest, with thrush-colored hair and olive aspect, rode the only grandchild of Liselotte Mehmel. Having stepped out onto the porch this afternoon to water her fuchsia, she watched the boy go past. Liselotte waved, but shook her head.

"Going home, going home," he called out to her, not stopping. Felix Mehmel was fourteen—with good and bad, everything, still to come—in the flat-calm summer of 1907. Arriving home, six blocks farther on, Felix took from behind the bicycle seat several books he had belted together and wedged there, while his mother regarded him from the front steps of the great house, consternation and delight mingling in a toss of her head.

"Felix Mehmel, are you going to spend your whole life just reading? I mean, just *reading* about everything?"

"Yes, ma'am."

He kissed away her frown, passed indoors and up the curving stair. An afternoon sun was spreading mullion shadows across the walls and onto the carpets. In the corner niche of the landing was a heavy milk-glass vase with harebells wound into a bouquet, Neevah's handiwork of the day before.

To the left and down the hall of the second floor was Felix's room. He flung open the door to find the brindle cat, Hildy by name, seated in a bar of light. Dispassionate, erect, she mewed once, more reproachful than friendly, and extended a simpering face to be stroked on her cheeks, scratched between her eyes.

"Stinker," Felix said, obliging.

Mrs. McClung, the cook, had been out to the

fishmonger that morning, and there would likely be a scrap of pickerel or fluke to grace Hildy's dinner bowl. Was this the knowledge in which she privately smiled? Year by year, Felix thought, she'd been swapping youth for omniscience.

He threw off his steel-rimmed spectacles, lay down on the bed, opened a calf-bound volume, its pages foxed and brittle, that he'd taken from the book belt. Far gone already in nearsightedness, he preferred nonetheless to read without glasses, relishing the pleasant retinal stress as he went, his nose all but touching the page.

> *Inur'd to suffer, and resolv'd to dare,*
> *The Fates, without my pow'r, shall be without my care.*
> *This let me crave—since near your grove the road*
> *To hell lies open, and the dark abode*
> *Which Acheron surrounds, th' innavigable flood;*
> *Conduct me thro' the regions void of light,*
> *And lead me longing to my father's sight.*

Like walnuts when the husks are green, and darken at your touch, he took the impress of the words. But were they in like case, he and Aeneas? Aeneas at least could remember. Felix's struggling recollection pitched up this or that fragment of his own father, but these did not cohere. The clove scent of toilet water, the violent reek of the slop bowl: a dead father was both. Also, the noise of coins in his trousers pocket. The old-style watch with its burr-headed winding stem. The mono-grammed fob on a length of black grosgrain. The pair of mutton chops, which were as nettle to your cheek. The sudden blaze of anger with never a warning. Even, once, the back of the hand . . .

Facts are facts. What has happened cannot be made not to have happened. A black rain fell, a rivening wind came on. An angry God rolled the waters of earth over Galveston seven Septembers before. Felix's father disappeared into that weather.

Leaving the boy to his abstraction, Hildy had taken a measured leap into the open drawer of the chifferobe, gazed blandly behind her, and begun to forage with her head buried and hindquarters bristling up. Bored suddenly—all Hildy's moods were at right angles to one another—she leapt to the bed and put her barbed tongue against the boy's cheek.

Walnuts, When the Husks Are Green

What had Gulf waters done with Aharon Mehmel? Did banqueting sharks pick him clean? Do the smooth-as-jade bones tumble in some distant surf? Or had the utter dark, below the deep, somehow—husbanded him?

It is reported that Jonah was not a perfect man either. But God furnished the great fish regardless. And Jonah supplicated God from its belly for three days and three nights. Then God spoke to the fish, and the fish vomited Jonah out on dry land. This is reported.

If three days alive in the belly of death, why not three years? If three years, why not six? Seven, why not? Why not Aharon Mehmel spat back whole into life? This question Felix did not dare to ask, but his dreams did. His dreams, unremembered by day, asked whether death might not be death after all but instead the great preserver. Like Jonah's fish . . .

"I'm out of sorts today," Felix told Hildy, sporting a new locution. "I'm restive, cross-grained, querulous." Such connoisseurship is what came of reading the dictionary straight through. His mother wondered if she oughtn't to take that book and throw it on the fire. Then perhaps he'd speak like other children. Fourteen years old and all of English had been through Felix Mehmel, a hankerer for the wizardry of words.

> *Look round the wood, with lifted eyes, to see*
> *The lurking gold upon the fatal tree:*
> *Then rend it off, as holy rites command;*
> *The willing metal will obey thy hand,*
> *Following with ease, if favor'd by thy fate,*
> *Thou art foredoom'd to view the Stygian state:*
> *If not, no labor can the tree constrain;*
> *And strength of stubborn arms and steel are vain.*

He closed his eyes and said aloud the first two couplets, then the second, and so on. By now it was not so much an undertaking as an instinct with him: he got things by heart. His learning was an appetite that grew by what it fed on. While still in taffety cuffs and collar he could recite the caesars from Gaius Julius to Romulus Augustulus. At ten he had sat down and mastered the names of all the lands of the earth along with their populations, natural resources, geographical features, mean annual precipitations, and etcetera. He was comprehensive, was Felix.

"Our boy got the mind of a sponge!" Neevah would inform marvelling grown-ups who came to call. With his contemporaries Felix was less successful. They didn't care about dynasties of China, explorers of the New World, prime ministers of England. No point in rattling off for them exportable produce of the Argentine pampas.

One morning near the end of the school term Wick Frawley, a freckle-faced setter-eyed boy who'd been held back a grade and was near sixteen, and had age and height if not intelligence to lord over his classmates, and was Felix's special tormentor, had blocked the door to the schoolroom and said, "Felix Mehmel, you walk like a girl!" He'd said it loud enough for everybody to hear, then demonstrated, prancing tiptoe in a circle with his arms expressively up. "Tippy Toes, that's your name." Everybody, even the one or two Felix thought were his friends, had heartily laughed.

Miss Claypoole, their teacher, had said, "Wick Frawley, you stop that this instant!" But not too sternly, it seemed to Felix. "And Felix Mehmel, *you* just quit provoking Wick. Ah, do please spare me your innocent looks, young man! I may have been born yesterday, but I stayed up all night, and I know that it requires two to make a situation!" Her bosom rose and fell with the great truth she'd uttered. "Boys and girls, take your seats!"

From his place in the second row, Wick kept turning around, first to wink and flutter his eyelids, then to brandish a fist. Felix passed a note up to him which read, in excellent Palmer method: *Let me alone, you Visigoth!*

Miss Claypoole broke off her instruction to declare that she would not tolerate the passing of notes in class. "Felix, Wick, to the cloakroom!" Everybody knew what that meant—a thrashing on the palms with her ruler. When the boys got to the unventilated cubicle, where a faint odor of sweat presided, Wick with narrowed eyes said, "After school, honeybunch."

Then entered Claypoole with terrible swift sword and shut the cloakroom door behind her.

Walnuts, When the Husks Are Green

Felix could recollect a time before he understood that adults are former children, that children grow up to be adults. There had been children and there had been adults, and nobody ever got any taller or older, and everybody in this perdurable arrangement was as happy as could be. Now, swiftly, the changes came upon him: hair sprouting where the body forks, arms and legs splaying out, duskiness arriving in the voice.

That afternoon of early summer, a week or so after Decoration Day, there had come a knock at his bedroom door. He was busy. He was reading. What was this bother? The door swung open to reveal— Wick Frawley.

"Hello, honeybunch."

The boldness of it dumbfounded Felix. Wick Frawley, here in the *sanctum sanctorum*? It was infamous. Summer meant not having to endure this tinhorn bully—his cretinous name-calling, his swaggering threats. On the last day of school Felix had tucked into Wick's satchel a little note which read: *Farewell, you thick and brutal ignoramus, you misbegotten clodpole, you dim-witted recreant!*

Not so dim, however, not such a clodpole, not so

thick that he was unable to figure out from whom the valediction came. "I told that old nigger woman downstairs me and you had some unfinished bidnis. I told her your marker's come due. She said mighty fine."

What he'd said to Neevah was something else entirely, something sugary polite. He'd inveigled Neevah into letting him up those stairs!

"Here in this pocket, I got me a stick knife. I use it very often. You know what for? Putting my mark on enemies. Sure, honeybunch. Right on their upper lip, so everybody can see, I write—WICK FRAWLEY WAS HERE. Shows up good."

"I haven't seen anyone with that on."

"Hee, hee," laughed Wick. "They all wear mustaches now. Have to."

"Well, I don't think I can grow a mustache." Felix wished to, but could not, disguise a quaver in his voice.

"That'll be your problem, honeybunch."

This Wick Frawley was a boy of no background, with a mother and father companionately married, as they say, meaning that neither church nor state had beheld their union. The Frawleys lived over to the north side, a sallow tow-haired common-law family of indeterminate size. Six or eight children could be seen of an afternoon to mope on the tumble-down front porch while in a yard choked with jimson weed a dozen or more aimlessly picked at one another. The truant officer had had to call more than once and carried appalling rumors back to town. He said the Frawley children fed from a trough, devil taking the hindmost. He said a state of nature obtained at that paintless ramshackle weatherboard house, the stronger offspring guarding their prerogatives while the weaker wasted away.

Felix had observed that the shoes Wick wore to school were out at the backs and had the tongues missing—erstwhile shoes. Also, that his clothes were sometimes too small and sometimes too big, and of an inevitable dirtiness. He didn't exactly stink; you could say he was piquant, odorous; you could say he smelled like geraniums. But it was the hands Felix most noticed—casehardened as those of a grown man. Felix did not wish to see, but saw, that these hands of his tormentor were very beautiful. Now Wick raised them, palms facing, in a gesture of mock conciliation. "Course, you can get yourself off the hook with me real quick like."

"By what means?"

"Hee, hee," laughed Wick. "You can fess up to being a girl inside them britches. Cause I don't put my mark on no girls, honeybunch."

To scream would be proof of what Wick alleged, so Felix did not let himself scream. Besides, that stick knife mightn't be an empty boast.

"Just take them britches down."

Whirling within himself, Felix said nothing, made no move.

"Lemme git a look, that's all," said Wick and whereas his voice had heretofore been all derision, now it harbored something different, a plea. "Lemme git a look." And the clenchfist of fear in which he held Felix was also, inexplicably, a caress. "Lemme." As in a dream Felix complied, not excluding the underdrawers.

"Aw, hell," said Wick, "I see a weener." And he pulled a mournful face. "What are we gonna do about that? Better kiss your elbow, I think. Sure, honeybunch! Kiss your elbow, change your sex, don't you know that?"

Walnuts, When the Husks Are Green

Trousers down around his shoes, Felix said, "Impossible."

"Aw, try."

Admittedly there are truths unlearnable from the reference works. Was this one of them? Felix puckered up, straining towards one unattainable elbow and then the other as something humble, without a name, broke forth in him, something with joy in it: the dreamlike satisfaction of doing just as Wick bade him.

"Your weener's strange."

"In what respect?" asked Felix, who had but the indistinct memory of his father's naked person to go on.

"Well, it ain't all there. I'll show you what a good one looks like."

Wick now took out the uncircumcised real thing. "Mine's better, ain't it?"

"Yours is better, Wick." But Felix avowed silently that Wick's was *not* better. It looked like a sad case. It looked like a finished bloom of morning glory. It looked—well, just not how it ought to.

Now Wick pushed his foreskin forward, pulled it back. Forward, back; he was changing size. "Too bad you can't do this!" Forward, back, ever more quickly. Felix had studied his own privates in all phases, even rubbed himself, with pleasurable results, against the bedclothes, the window seat, the hook-stitched rug. But Wick's method, this stalwart back and forth, was—Felix surmised —something new, a discovery all of Wick's own.

"Join my club," the latter said. His dread blue gaze had lost the glint of meanness. Tending thus ardently to himself, pumping away, sighing, Wick acquired innocence.

"What kind of club is it?" Felix asked.

"Real private."

"How many members?"

"Just me, so far," said Wick, and moaned. "You'll be second. But honeybunch, the dues is *steep*."

"How much, may I ask?"

"Three dollars," said Wick, and gave out a groan, and cracked a lovesome grin. "Hey, feature *that*," he said, using his free hand to point. "I believe I see a boner on you! I *do* believe I see a boner! . . . Do what I do . . . That's right."

The rusty pattern of freckles across Wick's nose, beheld hitherto as the very ensign of evil, seemed now but a handsome detail in a scheme of hand-someness. All malice, all mockery were gone from him. Beautiful and good, he forged ahead to his conclusion.

So, too, did Felix, following as best he could Wick's lead while, in the pulses, there rose a blood-boltered singing. He had a moment to wonder, was something irreplaceable about to go from him? Or was this deep source perpetual, bedded in the braving and original flesh? Yes, here in tumult lay the truth of truths, surpassing knowledge, granting the vital mean and measure.

Yes.

Outside, a cobalt light of day was sifting in through leaves of the sugarberry tree. Hildy at the windowsill had turned her back to the human scene, averted her gaze. Upon the uppermost bough of the sugarberry an eastern pewee was prinking himself. *Pee-ah-wee*, the bird sang, out of reach. A breeze shifted the canopy of leaves. *Pee-ah-wee*, the bird sang. Hildy's nostrils widened, Hildy lashed her tail. Grown old though she was, she leapt for the upper bough as sidewise through leafage the pewee darted away. Hildy gazed lornly after the bird, then cocked an ear forward. From treetop to treetop, through the surcharged afternoon, starting with the sugarberry and passing to the camphor and the osage orange, had risen a thrumming of locusts.

A whole other life, sweet and perilous, bloomed in the mind. Were Felix's accumulated school hurts, the torment of them laid up in memory, hereby to be annulled? Perennially outside, was he to pass in? Strange and delicious, the feeling of inclusion in a secret.

Wick said nothing, only wiped his hand against the tail of his shirt, and loured. Felix cast about nervously for a topic. "Are you a fancier of cats, Wick? I know I am. Just look at Hildy, out on a limb. I never tire of observing her, so dignified, so elegant. Others can keep their *canes familiares*, better known as dogs. That's my opinion. What's yours, Wick?"

"My opinion is, you owe me three dollars."

"Pardon? Oh yes, certainly, the dues. I'm afraid I haven't got them just now, but most assuredly will by next week."

"You ain't in good standing till I get them three dollars."

Walnuts, When the Husks Are Green

"I certainly am eager to be in good standing."

Now Wick hitched up his pants in one motion. "Don't tell nobody about none of this, you hear? *Nobody*," he emphasized, gaining the door, and with a rakehell backward glance was gone.

CHAPTER FOUR

Track of the Moon

L ISELOTTE had fought her younger son hard when he declared his intention to take rooms at the Tremont House.

"A thirty-seven-year-old man needs his privacy," he told her.

"A thirty-seven-year-old man needs a *wife!*" she replied.

His lodgings were simple: a bedroom and a den with a portière hung between. Here he spent the changeless days filling a copper trough at his windowsill with dried fruit and hemp seed and millet, waiting to see what species would come to feed, noting them down in his bird ledger. There were

the dusky seaside sparrow, the white-breasted nut-
hatch, the black-crested titmouse, the blue gros-
beak; several kinds of junco; the cardinal, the
magpie, the catbird, the starling, the Inca dove, the
grackle, the cedar waxwing. There was the painted
bunting, beautiful beyond words. Also, the hooded
oriole and the orange-crowned warbler. Two win-
ters ago Leo had put suet in the feeders and
attracted a covey of green jays, far north of their
usual transit.

Sometimes imagination—or longing—got the
better of him. He would swear to have seen at his
window the Antillean palm swift, though this could
not be. Or heard the corncrake shouting his famous *too-far-to-FLEE! too-far-to-FLEE!*

Hard upon a peremptory knock, Liselotte Mehmel strode in. "Who are Munger and Roache?" she
wanted to know. "I've just come from the office. I
see you've made out bank drafts, large ones, to a
Peter Munger and an Albert Roache."

"Mama—"

"You have your rights, of course. It is not my
business how you squander what you have come
into. Feed it to the birds, bankroll whom you

choose! Some generations make, others spend. Good; I accept. Go right to the bottom of the barrel—Aharon's not here to stop you." But here she desisted, for this was unfair according to an axiom debarring comparisons between elder and younger—the moreso now that one of them was dead.

Leo was tall, pigeon-chested, nervously thin. Looking at him you got a poor impression. And yet secreted within Liselotte's reticence about Aharon's superiority was a second and deeper reticence, belying the first: of two boys, one of whom shone like gold, she loved better the one who had not. This afternoon she'd found him in his preferred at-home gear, a silk dressing gown embroidered with the moon and stars. Leo pushed to one side books and papers covering the horsehair divan and urged her to sit down, he would order up tea.

"No, thank you, *liebling*." She paced to the window, shaking her head. "Let me tell you about the true state of our affairs. We are encumbered, do you understand? Rich people? We are not rich."

As ever when finances were mentioned, Leo's face composed itself into an Asiatic remoteness.

Now his mother drew in a breath to expound further her theme, but gave it up. "You must be more prudent. That is all I've come to say." She turned to go, then faltered, turning back to him with something new in her voice. "Except that I think you look pale for this month of the year. You've stopped too much indoors."

"Mama, don't go yet. I've something to show you." Leo knelt down and with care brought from under his reading desk something fragile and bony, draped with a foulard he ceremoniously pulled away to reveal—a pterodactyl-like form, canvas attached under the little cambered wing ribs and stitched around spanwise wooden slats. He explained: "This is a model of the monoplane glider the great Otto Lilienthal constructed from waxed cotton and peeled willow wands, took to a high place in the Rhinower Hills, fastened to his person—"

"He'll break his neck!"

"He did, he did." Leo stared at the little mechanism, testing one by one with his forefinger the taut wooden ribbings. "You can't imagine how happy I am to own this."

"I'm happy for you. Also sad, if you like, for Lilienthal."

"He was the world's greatest aeronaut—so far, I
mean."

"Sorry, *liebling*, not to know." Her kiss to either
cheek. She was gone.

Leo went into the bedroom, lay down supine,
folded rawboned hands across his pigeon chest.
Would it work? he wondered. A small fortune had
already gone to the boys for materials. Admittedly
these were not the Montgolfiers, not the Wrights of
recent fame. These were Albert Roache and Peter
Munger, Catholic boys from another part of town
who were minded to build a heavier-than-air craft,
a biplane glider of their own design.

Three weeks previous they had spotted Leo
mooning along the sea wall in dimity plus fours and
bare feet, his long scarf playing in the wind behind
him. A molly-mop, they could see at once. A nancy
man, a spooney. He'd been casting sheep's eyes
their way but left off now in favor of two long-billed
curlews, largest and noblest of shorebirds, that
wheeled and banked in the rich afternoon sun.
Shielding an upturned gaze with one hand, he took

from his pants pocket a handful of sunflower seed with the other and pitched it down onto the shingle. Amid the immediate squawkings and bellyachings of gulls and the *kak-kak-kak* of terns Leo could hear, musical, the dignified iamb of the sicklebills: *cur-LEW! cur-LEW!* Now they descended, driving back the smaller birds. Folding their wings over cinnamon-pale underplumage, the curlews settled down to the scattered feed, grasping it with long arched bills, tossing their heads up blithely, expertly.

"Hey, mister! . . . Mister! . . . *You!*" Me? Leo asked himself. He had tried his best to cadge a friendly glance from those two youths seated beneath a grass-grown dune up the beach; but then had turned away, for their smiles did not look friendly. What now? They wanted to harrow him a little? Probably.

"Hey, mister." Speaking was the taller of the two, black Irish, sunburned over fair skin. The other hung back. "Roache is the name, Albert Roache. Me and my friend," he said, gesturing over one shoulder with a thumb, "we're, uh, well sir, we're what I guess you'd call—bird fanciers ourselves.

Could not help but notice your way just then with that pair of big ones."

"Curlews."

"Yes sir, right you are!" He looked back and with an upswing of the arm summoned his sulky associate. "This here's Peter Munger."

He was square-built and powerful, was Munger, and with cornflower eyes and a way of tossing the suntanned forelock back from them. Leo ran both hands nervously down his shirt front as if to brush away crumbs, extended his hand, said, "I'm Leo Mehmel." A could-mean-anything smile played over Munger's lips and was gone. He clasped Leo's hand, said hello.

Peter and Albert were bicycle mechanics who, in the five cool Galveston months, inhabited tiny quarters above their boss Mr. Fewtrell's repair shop in Post Office Street. Both had worked there since abandoning school at the finish of eighth grade. But what they called home through the long stretch of warm months was a knurled, venerable live oak to the west of town, out past the corporate limit. Peter and Albert styled themselves lovers of the free air and, to show they were serious, had

built their dwelling in a tree—constructing it more-
over to look like an aeroplane, uncanny to behold,
for it seemed to have flown right into the craggy
arms and stuck fast there.

Alone and aloft in the upper reaches they did
not address each other by their paltry baptismal
names; preferring to borrow a little glory, it was
"Orville," it was "Wilbur." Thus they spent their lei-
sure—in dreams. They drew up the yellow-pine
rungs of the rope ladder, their umbilical down to
earth, and contrived an empire out of nothing, out
of air.

Poor Leo's knees had trembled ungovernably
when first he made the ascent. He got short of
breath, had to pause at the eighth rung. "Too weak
to climb a damn rope ladder!" snorted Munger
under his breath. Holding the cords taut from
below for him, stifling peals of laughter, grimacing
so that the tendons stood out on their necks, Albert
and Peter shook their witty heads in despair. They
watched him hoist at last through the square
entrance cut in the floor, barking his shins as he
went, then scrabbled up behind him. Leo had only
a moment alone in the treehouse. He saw the

bound-up sleeping rolls, the spirit lamp, the little mirror with a distorting bend in the glass, the pair of automobile goggles dangling from a nail, the furled mosquito nets, the ten or twelve aeronautical models suspended from slats overhead.

"Make yourself to home," Roache said, beaming.

Leo was still lightheaded, catching his breath. His shins hurt. "I've never been in a treehouse before."

"Yea, I'll bet you *ain't*," said Munger, and flashed the give-nothing smile. Immediately, he'd opened three bottles of Moxie, poured off half of each, filled them back up with rye, and now handed one to Leo and one to Roache. "Happy days, gentlemen," he gravely said.

Leo put up his bottle so that it rang against the other two. A pretty sound.

They drank.

"Hear that?" said Roache. "Every evening about now the locusts get off work and the crickets come on." It was true. The fretful heated din had given way to a silvery chirring. Into western stands of cumulus the last of day flashed up. The sky to eastward was a scumbled blue.

"I have to be going," Leo said.

Neither seemed to hear. Munger drank his Moxie and rye in silence. Roache lit the spirit lamp, unfurled the mosquito nets.

"I think that I have to be going."

Roache pulled the floor hatch to. "Have a look at this," he said, reaching outside the net for one of the aeroplane models. "This is the Lilienthal glider." He told the story of the great aviator's bravery and death.

Followed a silence, only the crickets cheeping. "Can't say as I hold with all this wanting to fly," Leo said at last. "That's for the birds." He laughed a little at his own *plaisantrie*, even tried on a grin. Munger shot Roache a dolorous look.

"What I mean is, people are going to get hurt. Birds are different from us, you know. They've got the right ratio of body weight to muscular power. We don't."

"It ain't a question of weight, Mr. Mehmel, and it ain't a question of power," Roache parried, with due respect. "It's a question of the right *application* of power." He explained how a craft sustains itself, by the slipstream it makes in the air. And there was authority in this; Roache's voice sounded manly, considering.

"Would you actually try it yourselves?"

"Damn right!" swanked Munger, and tossed back the last of his Moxie and rye.

Roache explained: "We want to try it, yes, but only when we're sure we got a sound design. Then there's the matter of building it proper." He inhaled sharply to disguise a tremor in his breathing. It was his moment. "That's where you come in, Mr. Mehmel."

"Beg pardon?"

"Well, sir . . . we need us a sponsor."

"*Money*," said Munger, for emphasis. "I ain't risking my neck in some crate what ain't built right. We need the best materials. And those cost what I said—money."

"What makes you so sure you'll know what to do once you're up there?" asked Leo.

For answer, Munger yawned.

"Oh, Pete here'll be a first-class aviator," said Roache. "He's had piloting experience—in a motorcar, I admit, but the principle's the same."

Track of the Moon

All over Galveston Island, at this hour, in this month, there commenced the pulse of fireflies, greenish gold, which was a signal. It meant there were mosquitoes, too. Here the home-thrust of the climate carried fevers: yellow, dengue. A mosquito, hereabouts, could kill a man.

"I expect you'd better stay the night," Albert said to Leo, unfastening a third sleeping roll and spreading it a little way from his own and Peter's. "We keep us a slop jar up here," he said. "We don't on no account go down to the field after dark. Not this time of year."

Munger was listing quick into sleep, an idle finger plunged into the empty Moxie bottle. His jaw hung slack, his breath came in fits and starts. Amazing how little liquor it took to fell him. Now and then he would absently raise his free hand to scratch himself behind the ear or under the nose.

Roache spoke low. "Two summers ago, Pete's girl, Grace Ellen Deweese, she died. It was the fever, Mr. Mehmel—you remember that bad spell of it went through the island? Well, durn if Pete hadn't taken her out on a long drive to the country, and the hour got late, and the sun went down on them, and there they were in an open cart, ate up alive."

The liquor had made Roache garrulous.

"Of course, the Deweeses and the Mungers never did care for each other. Pete and Grace Ellen, they was engaged but had to keep it a secret."

Roache turned down the spirit lamp to barely a glint, then settled back, cut himself a chew of the rich black leaf he favored.

"Want some?"

"No thank you, Albert."

He returned the tobacco pouch and knife to his trousers pocket. "Well, Pete and Grace Ellen both got real sick. And Grace Ellen wasn't too strong to begin with. Delicate kind of girl. On the day she died, Mrs. Deweese showed up over to the Mungers' and hollered into the sickroom, 'I hope you die too, Peter Munger! You done killt my Grace Ellen and I hope you die!' Mrs. Munger took out after Mrs. Deweese shouting, 'Witch, keep off my boy! Keep off my boy, witch!' I was standing across the street, I seen it all. I'll tell you something else,

Mr. Mehmel," he said, his voice now down to a whisper. "Pete and Gracc Ellen, they was very deep in love. I mean, as close as two *can* be, if you get my meaning. He don't talk about her no more, don't ever even mention her name. I asked him why and he offered to button my lip if I asked him again. I'm embarrassed to tell where he goes now every payday. Not out on the town with some nice girl, not on your life! He slinks off to Crummer's, which a fine gentleman such as yourself probably ain't never even heard of. It's a pleasure housc, Mr. Mehmel." Roache chewed his plug sidewise, looking meditative.

"Yes, Albert, as I know."

"You? *You* know?" Roache eyed Leo doubtfully.

"By reputation," Leo explained. "Not through any first-hand experience."

"Oh, uh, same here," Roache put in. "What I know's strictly through the reputation—which is pretty *gamey*, ain't it, Mr. Mehmel? They got some little holes in the walls over there, and for six bits you can watch a gal undress, right down to her underthings, and then for another six she takes those off, too. Mighty fine sight, so I understand. Then for *big* spenders they got these here privays, they're called. Little rooms not big enough for more than a bed. No ceilings to them, Mr. Mehmel, just chicken wire so as to stop you peeping over from one to the next. You can *hear* some mighty peculiar things."

Roache paused, looking reluctant, but also eager, to go on.

"For example?" Leo helpfully asked.

"For example, Mayor W. T. 'Pappy' Critchmar, getting it better than he can take, howling his fool head off. Oh, yeah! I heard it all."

"Then, you've been there."

"Come to think of it, sir, I have been—once— and it absolutely was Mayor Critchmar I heard shouting, 'Oh yeah, oh yeah' and 'dawlin' and 'sugar' and screaming, 'You can have *all* my money!' Then he quieted down."

"That's shocking, Albert, I must say."

"Ain't it, though?"

The crickets chirred now at a swifter interval, drunk with their hue and cry. Munger had settled into an equable steady snoring. Far off, a fog horn began to sound.

"Mind if I ask, Mr. Mehmel—how old are you?"

A pause. "Twenty-eight."

This fell as readily from Leo's lips as if it were truth, for on that June night, winsome and mild, it seemed as if life were hastening towards him, not drawing away. His real age, thirty-seven, simply did no justice to what he felt so he dispensed with it, becoming—presto—twenty-eight.

"And yourself, Albert?"

"Me, I'm twenty-one, soon be twenty-two."

A lengthy pause, the crickets singing. Roache smiled sedately. "Twenty-one, nothing done."

Leo contemplated the rhyme. "Twenty-two, still to do," he proffered in return.

Immediately, it was a game between them. "Twenty-three —" said Roache, then faltered.

"Hard alee," Leo submitted. An excellent rhyme.

"Twenty-four, back for more!" Roache rejoined, delighted with himself, grinning away.

"Twenty-five, still alive." This Leo instantly repented of. It was too obvious.

"Twenty-six, took my licks," said Roache, gaining ground. He liked this game.

"Twenty-seven, nearer to heaven."

"Twenty-eight, twenty-eight . . ." Roache faltered, Roache was stumped.

But there was a light in Mehmel's eyes. "Twenty-eight, rose to the bait," he tendered majestically.

Laughter. A gratified silence, smiles lingering out.

"You're going to help us, ain't you?"

Leo nodded slowly, ruefully, still smiling. "How much do you need?"

"Four hundred—the whole ball of wax." Roache stared hard, looking for an assent. "Here's how I break it down, sir." He took a sheet of foolscap from his hip pocket and unfolded it for Leo to see. "We need us good strong birch wood for the spars. And China silk for air foils. And plenty of cable, for guy lines. The mechanical parts can be pulled out of some old bikes we already got."

"Bicycles?" asked Leo, disbelieving.

"Sure. Bicycles was a good enough beginning for Orville and Wilbur, don't you know? When we heard they used to be bike mechanics, no different from us, I said, 'Petey boy, we'll do ourselves as proud.'"

"But why do again what's already been done?"

"It won't be the same," Roache said in the considering voice of a few minutes before, the voice of the last word. "It won't be the same because it won't *be* Wilbur and Orville, it'll be me and Pete." And to this there was nothing to answer. Both listened now to the noisy largo of Munger breathing. Roache pulled off the sleeper's shoes, lugged him forward by the feet till he lay supine, placed a change of clothing under his head. Best to leave him lie; it was too warm for sleeping rolls anyhow. Roache folded his own for a pillow, advising Leo to do the same.

"Do we have your word, Mr. Mehmel?"

"You do, Albert."

Roache leaned forward to extinguish the spirit lamp, and as he did it shone on his face, gold suddenly and shadowed blue, for that fractional second not the face of a young man but of an old woman. Then Roache recovered his face of youth.

He quenched the spirit lamp. Through spaces

between the slats, through mosquito netting, were stars and the slow track of the moon, that night only a sliver, faint, hung up in summer fog.

"Good night, Mr. Mehmel."

"Good night, Albert."

CHAPTER FIVE

Winnie Street

FELIX MEHMEL spent the better part of June trying to raise three dollars. He applied to the gardener, Filipe, naked to the waist and turning the earth where Lucy's hollyhocks had flourished a summer ago. He appealed to McClung, whom he found making an inventory of the pantry. "Just hand me, if you please, those Mason jars," she said from the second rung of her step ladder. McClung put up currant jam and apple butter and greengage marmalade, pickled radishes and gooseberry catsup, all according to closely held receipts which had come down to her from an Irish mother, now deceased. They were written out in the maternal hand onto back pages of an old-style latch-and-key cashbook which when Felix was younger McClung would sometimes let him look into. Back in Galway her mother had made a living from the sale of these comestibles, guarding the knowledge of how to prepare them as jealously as she'd reckoned up her profits.

"Three dollars? Get along with you," said McClung.

Out on the back gallery, fanning herself with a broken-down leghorn, drawing the labored elderly breaths in and out, sat Neevah, nobody's idea of an easy touch. She barely turned her head for answer to Felix's imploration.

He let the screen door slam behind him and pedalled off to the house of Miss Murph and Miss Truley.

Miss Etta Mae Murph and Miss Velma Truley were two women who had slept in one bed for thirty years. When the day broke on their little house in Winnie Street, the two of them were quickly about. Miss Murph hastened to her desk to correct a copybook or prepare a lesson. Miss Truley fell to and made their breakfast (usually nothing more than hot black coffee and a buckwheat porridge). Sometimes Miss Truley would inquire sonorously from her post at the cookstove what Miss Murph would like to eat for lunch, and Miss Murph would holler back, "Lunch is only eaten from a pail," correcting Miss Truley, for the noonday meal was more properly called "dinner."

Miss Truley would throw open the back screen door and call out for Bob, their lop-eared hound. "Bob-*by!*" And Bob would leap up from the cool sandy sleeping pit he had dug himself behind the photinia. Into the kitchen he would hurry, humble and abashed, a dog of no particular breed or even color, wagging what there was of his tail. "Hello, Bobby boy."

Poor devil, he'd been wrongly dealt with as a pup. It was a thing that bewildered them to think about: for fun, somebody, some person, had cut off Bob's ears and snapped his tail and put him out to die. He was near bled to death when Miss Truley, passing by an alley off Church Street, had heard the faint piteous cries from behind a row of dust bins. Somebody had mutilated a baby dog and thrown him out with the garbage.

When Truley got Bob home, cowled in a bloody kerchief, Miss Murph took a look and learnedly declared his name to be Zopyrus; but Truley said no, his name was Bob . . .

The front parlor where Miss Murph, a tutor in Greek, Latin, mathematics, geography and history, met with her pupils had an upright piano the ladies had rented with an option to buy and paid for in installments. Above it, something funny hung on the parlor wall. An old ferrotype of the two of them taken at the Dallas Fair and Exposition when they were scarcely more than girls, standing with plenary smiles and arms identically akimbo in front of the great Ferris wheel. But someone had painted over the photograph, giving them black knitted shawls and gray hair and big crow's-feet at the corners of their eyes and mouths—hundred-fifty-year-old women!—and indeed the joke legend beneath the picture read: *Etta Mae and Velma at the Millennium.*

Felix had arrived for his afternoon lesson a little early. He let himself in without knocking, as he'd been told to, hung up his cap on the clothes tree in the vestibule, and pussyfooted to the kitchen.

"Smells good, Miss T."

Quick as you please she had sliced him a helping of the best apple charlotte in south Texas and soused it with cream. "What's your lesson?" she asked, a surprising question from Truley, who preferred other things to books.

"It's Virgil, the underworld visit—"

"Well, I never can keep all those stories straight," she said over her shoulder. "Course Miss Murph has told me all of them one time or other. While we're waiting to fall asleep, Miss Murph tells me stories."

Rarely had Felix seen this woman's hands at rest. They kneaded the dough or took the husks off of corn; they stoked a fire or rinsed the dishes or coaxed the dirt out of a corner; they cut broadcloth or muslin or gingham according to the store-bought patterns, and gathered the cloth into furbelows, and sewed the fine seams.

"Oh, you smart people are too much for me," she went on with her back to him. "Now take Miss Murph. Story's never just a story to her. She's got to

· 79 ·

go twisting it this way and that—wringing it out, you know, for what it might *mean*. Phooey! I fold my arms and say, 'Etta Murph, you leave that story alone!' Way I figure, if it's a good story there's nothing more to say when it's finished. Right? So you start your story; we'll see if I remember it or not." She wiped her hands front and back against her apron and joined him at the table.

Felix laid down his fork. He smoothed the hair from his forehead. He locked his feet into the chair rungs. "Aeneas must found Rome," he put it to her, just as Miss Murph had put it to him. The words were as yet too large, of course, a hand-me-down he would need time to grow to. "Aeneas must found Rome, though his heart wants other things. The prophetess"—this he pronounced in Miss Murph's way, putting slack into the middle vowel— "the prophetess has told him he'll win through. What he asks is to go down to the dead and see his father again. The prophetess says that only love can get him there and back."

Warming to the song, Felix had risen and walked a semicircle around the table, then halted, laid one hand gravely to his heart. Miss Truley sat smiling and shut-eyed.

"He must pluck the golden bough where it glitters in the gloom," he said, but here left off, for though Miss Murph had come silently into the kitchen as he stood with his back to the doorway and his hand to his breast, he knew that she, a woman believing the point of life is to become wise about life, was standing there behind him.

"To work!"

Felix turned to see her tapping at the lapel watch worn on her gingham shirtwaist. She had perceived a sloughing off in this her prize pupil, who seemed lately to have things on his mind other than the hortatory subjunctive. Today she'd wring his withers till he got it right.

They entered the front parlor, seated themselves side by side at Murph's desk, and opened *Aeneidos*, by Publius Vergilius Maro.

"Where were we last time?" Murph asked.

"Right here," said Felix and pointed to each word in turn: ". . . *sate sanguine divum, Tros Anchisiade, facilis descensus Averno.*"

"Translate, please."

He studied the words for a few seconds, then felt the gooseflesh rise. Felix said: "It is easy to die."

"More literally, Felix," Murph replied with a grimace, but with a smile, too, in one corner of her mouth. "Kindred by blood to the gods—" she began in order to help him.

"Kindred by blood to the gods . . . Trojan son of Anchises . . . the way down . . . the way down . . . from Avernus . . . is very easy," Felix translated, and looked up brightly from the page.

"*Noctes atque dies patet atri ianua Ditis*," declared Murph.

"Night and day . . . the doorway . . . of Dis . . . stands open."

"Indeed, it does," Murph affirmed. "*Sed revocare gradum superasque evadere ad auras*," she blazoned now at the boy, "*hoc opus, hic labor est*."

Felix took a fresh grip on his chair. "But . . . to, uh, revoke your steps—"

"To *retrace* your steps . . ."

"To retrace your steps . . . back up to . . . to . . . the upper air?"

"That's right . . ."

"Here is . . . the work . . . here, the task."

Murph popped a horehound lozenge into her mouth and handed one to Felix. This in order to fortify themselves for bringing over from the sublime Latin how much love and desire you need to cross Stygian water twice, and twice to look into eternal night of Tartarus. And then came a smoothness into the boy's brow, for they had reached the part he'd swatted up special to please Miss Murph. He had it by heart from the Dryden translation, found on his own while bookworming at the Galveston Island Public Library. Full-voiced, Felix sent the rhymed couplets sounding now through the little house and caused Truley in the next room to put down her crewel work and listen.

> *. . . thick woods and gloomy night*
> *Conceal the happy plant from human sight.*
> *One bough it bears; but (wondrous to behold!)*
> *The ductile rind and leaves of radiant gold:*
> *This from the vulgar branches must be torn,*
> *And to fair Proserpine the present borne,*
> *Ere leave be giv'n to tempt the nether skies.*
> *The first thus rent, a second will arise . . .*

And he might have carried on for some lines more, but Miss Murph clucked her tongue, shook her head. "Showboat! Showboat!"

For near two hours they kept up this good work, translating up to the part where Aeneas, notable for piety, reaches the maw of Avernus and observes two doves, an omen, settle in the top of a two-colored tree. "*Discolor unde auri per ramos aura refulsit*," Murph pronounced. And Felix replied that in and upon the green boughs there shone a golden glitter that was different; that just as mistletoe is vivid against the sere and gray of winter, so showed leaves of thin gold against the dark ilex, and rattled dryly in the breeze; that though the glittering tendril resisted him, Aeneas stalwartly broke it off to carry back to the Sibyl's lair.

Afternoon was declining now, casting light higher up the parlor wall, letting through a welcome stir of air. Felix shrugged his shoulders against a stiffness coming on, threw his head side to side, took off the steel-rimmed spectacles to rub his eyes. Miss Murph rubbed her eyes too.

In their singleheartedness of study they had not heard Harvey P. Runge arrive by the back door.

Winnie Street

"Iceman here," he said unemphatically through the screen. "You girls be wanting some?"

He was florid, jug-eared, familiar as you please. But was Miss Truley intimidated by ilk of him? She moseyed to the back door, said, "Harvey P. Runge" (pronounced his way, to rhyme with sponge), "how long in the teeth are we going to have to get before you stop calling us *girls*? Don't answer that, Harvey, just cut me half a cake. Also, if you please, a bag of shavings."

The which she uses for iceing two tall glasses of pear cider. And on soft feet brings them into the sunlit parlor. "For the scholars!" she announces, but the scholars do not turn around, not yet. They just sit there, honor-bent, staring at words, as the book-besotted have always sat and stared, bent in body and mind over work, making much of the little they are given to know.

CHAPTER SIX

No End of Trouble

"NO END OF TROUBLE," said Lucy Mehmel beneath her breath. This was an acquired trick of the heart and mind. If she felt herself giving way to a hope, she pronounced the remedial words: No—end—of—trouble.

Seated in a window of the sun parlor, she'd napped away the shank end of that afternoon, Hildy purling beside her. When Felix got home from Miss Murph's he slid open the pocket doors wide enough to wiggle a beckoning finger at the cat and shape her name on his lips, but her only response was to nudge one eye deeper into Lucy's bodice.

Go back to your spinster girlfriends, said a voice that stood for Hildy in his head. Taking two at a time the steps to the second landing, he told himself that her impudence had gotten out of hand.

Lucy still wore her bloodstone ring with the Pumphrey scutcheon etched in reverse. Certainly, there had been the provocation for taking it off. Her hardset ill-considering father had cast this best of daughters from his door. When she brought the Jew to New Orleans for apprisement, Mr. Pumphrey's sallow eyes were quick about it. She could have her beer-brewing money-loving deicide, he told her, or she could have her father. Not both.

Powerless against her husband, Mrs. Pumphrey had wept, had railed. No use. The familial cup was filled with gall; her lot was to drink, loyally and deep. Two years ago, after nearly fourteen of silence, Lucy had received a telegram from New Orleans. "Father died today"—that and nothing more. But by the next mail came a real letter with all the dammed-up feelings turned loose. "He forbid your sister and me to write you," Mrs. Pumphrey wrote. "As for Neevah he said it was good riddance to a bad nigger. He just stopped being himself—calling Neevah bad like that. He told us you were the same as dead but late nights we heard the drunk sobs come through his door. Oh I am not a clever woman but Luce I figured out a way of going on. When we heard tell of Galveston any little thing Daddy would start working his jaw real mean like but me in my mind I saw the fine little town and in a glass coach my Lucy . . ."

Upon their betrothal Aharon Mehmel wanted to accompany his intended to speak with Rabbi Nathan Gernsbacher—a rather solemn talk about conversion to the Jewish faith—but Gernsbacher had insisted that the young lady come on her own. It was his bounden rabbinical duty to try to dissuade her.

Gernsbacher had attended the great seminary at Breslau, where he learned to dress and groom himself like any other man but to go on thinking and feeling and conducting himself like a Jew. In the traditional beard and forelocks he would have been a more persuasive-looking rabbi, Lucy felt.

Cleanshaved, he had a polecat look about him.
But you forgot this as soon as he spoke, for
Gernsbacher said exalted things—confounding
and inspiring the girl, as if a tongue of fire were
talking. "Does not grace seem a comelier thing to
you than obligation, Miss Pumphrey? You understand, don't you, that the Jew knows only obligation
where your present religion invokes grace? And
that this obligation is to a God without personality,
or image, or name?" Gernsbacher was sweating
under the glazed shirt and celluloid collar; wet
rings showed at the armpits of his pongee suit. He
glared at her with shopworn eyes. Beneath the
four-in-hand necktie, his heart was beating hard.
"Anybody, Miss Pumphrey, can speak the name of
the man Jesus, speak it aloud as if it were his own;
but the name of the God of Sinai will be a secret
until the end of the world." Now he took out a
handkerchief, mopped his brow and his baldness.
He looked away from her, then looked her in the
eye. "We are instructed that one is better off not to
have been born at all, Miss Pumphrey, than to try to
guess at that end of days—how or when it will be."

No use, these monitions. After eight months

of reading Scripture with him, of partaking of the days of feasting and fasting, of distinguishing between what is commanded and what is forbidden, even of learning to pronounce a little of the arduous Hebrew language and to extoll God in the poetry of it, Miss Lucy Pumphrey, formerly of New Orleans, had entered the ritual bath and become a Jewess.

Down Broadway this afternoon toiled an elderly fishmonger behind his two-wheel cart. Lucy heard the hawking call—red fish on offer, trout, sardines, flounder, mackerel—new notes in the midst of her old familiar dream, which was this:

The Jews are in their synagogue. Struck dumb in his eloquence, Gernsbacher stands before them, listens to the breaching elements. He finds his tongue at last, tells them that, yes, the Lord is passing by, and a great and strong wind is rending the rocks before the Lord. But the Lord is not in the wind.

A turkey buzzard, desperate for shelter, comes through the open casement. He flaps his nasty wings and circles the sanctuary once and settles atop the high back of Gernsbacher's mahogany chair. With cognate eyes and matched frowns the two of them, buzzard and man, stare at the congregation. Gernsbacher puts out his hands for silence, he will speak. Everyone listens, the buzzard too. After the wind an earthquake, says Gernsbacher; but the Lord is not in the earthquake. After the earthquake, a fire; but the Lord is not in the fire. Not in the wind, not in the earthquake, not in the fire! The Jews cry out on their absconded God. The buzzard when he hears them lumbers with a groan into the air . . .

"Wake up, sugar. They's company for you." This was Neevah talking, her spectacles up across the brow of a calico headcloth. At the doorway of the front parlor stood rabbi himself, looking older than in Lucy's dream, looking harassed and pale. Hildy hissed briefly, then disappeared under a lowboy. "Naughty!" Lucy said with a clap of her hands.

"Cats," Gernsbacher informed her, taking a seat in the armchair opposite, "are incapable of shame. My mother of blessed memory kept cats, more than you could count. If a cupboard or a closet you opened, there would be three or four of them,

yawning and stretching. It was a surprise, you
think, for us to come upon a lady cat with her newborn under an eiderdown or in a basin? It was no
surprise. Mama spoke wrathfully against them—
said they had acquired airs under her roof, fancied
themselves too good to eat rodents."

"She didn't turn them out?" Lucy asked.

"Unthinkable." Here rabbi paused, knowing
himself on a thin edge. Even after her conversion,
which was carried out in strict accordance, he had
continued to think of Lucy as gentile. Of course he
had. And Judaism, the real Judaism, was a burden
of secrets, tales one did not carry. How to tell her
that sins persist from one life to the next, that souls
of men and women are lodged in dogs and cats,
jackals and mice, rattlesnakes and scorpions, that
even the tree and the mineral stone cry out, if you
could but hear, with human syllables, if you could
but hear, for pity of God?

Oh, better not to tell her.

"Mama had succumbed to what I believe you call
an old wives' tale." Gernsbacher turned half his
mouth up in a smirk. "I am sorry to say she could
believe that illiterate nonsense—sinners doing

their penance in the bodies of cats! Why, the great Saadiah Gaon, may the memory of a *zaddik* be blessed, has refuted such rubbish for good and all." He rubbed his hands together over iced coffee Neevah had set down between them; he made a noise of delight, or tried to. But bile of falsehood rose in his throat.

"Rabbi," Lucy said, "I've wanted to tell you for a long time now . . . I've had it on my mind . . . You know, I have backslid. All you taught I seemed to forget as soon as I learned it. Just would not stay with me. And I found myself going back to what I knew. The very morning of my conversion, rabbi—please do not despise me when I tell you this—that very morning I shut my eyes and said a prayer to Mary. Yes, rabbi, the Blessed Virgin—who said she perfectly well understood. The day Felix was born I talked to her and she said it was fine for him to be, you know—circumcised. The day of the storm, there we were in the upstairs of the synagogue, you remember, cold and scared and everybody praying as hard as they could, and who should take a seat beside me but the Mother of God. That's right, rabbi. And she told me, 'Child, your husband is dead.' But she told me not to be afraid. She said Jesus on the Cross had already suffered everything we've got to suffer. She said, really, Jesus was *still* on the Cross and there He'd have to stay until there's no more of pain left anywhere on this earth. At the right hand of the Father? In glory? Oh, if you like, she said. A way of putting it, she said. But she said Christ is the power *because* He's the pain—still there, still there on His Cross, you see. Well, I said so many Hail Marys I lost the count of them. To myself, of course. It would just have looked to you like I was praying to your Jewish God—your *hard-of-hearing* Jewish God."

Gernsbacher stiffened. It was most unnecessary, he felt, this rubbing of the rabbinical nose in an alien creed. And did she even have its tenets right? Was it really the Church of Rome whose part she was speaking? Or had she garbled Christianity, making herself into a congregation of one? Soon as the occasion allowed, he would have a critical look at that so-called New Testament in order to see.

"My dear Lucy . . ." He paused in search of the formula that would dishonor neither of them. "We are all of us children of Abraham." Yes, this was foursquare, this was irreproachable. Pride of profession for a moment claimed Gernsbacher. His late mother would excuse him anything—wouldn't she?—hearing such a silver tongue at work. He would employ it to bring Lucy back to the fold; it would be easy.

Or so he thought. But caution now had fallen from her like all one garment. "I believe in God the Father almighty, Creator of heaven and earth," she informed him, "and in Jesus Christ, His only Son our Lord—"

Oh, shame.

"—who was conceived by the Holy Spirit, born of the Virgin Mary, suffered under Pontius Pilate—"

"Idolatry! Idolatry!" Gernsbacher told her.

"—was crucified, died, and was buried; he descended into hell; the third day he rose again—"

"Crucified gods! Virgin goddesses!"

"—rose again from the dead; he ascended into heaven, sits at the right hand of God the Father almighty—"

"Pagan *swill!* Idolatry!"

"From there He shall come to judge the quick and the dead."

Wearily, Gernsbacher reached for the glass of coffee Neevah had set down before him, took a long drink. "It is about Felix I have come to call," he said now, brooking no more nonsense. "Felix, I believe, has turned fourteen. His father was a Jew; his mother was and is—formally—a Jewess." Here he held up a forfending hand. "We will say so, for purposes of argument. It is time Felix read from the Scroll of the Law. It is past time he became, as we say, a *bar mitzvah*, a son of the commandment. This is what it means, you will remember: son of the commandment."

Lucy gave her head a shake. Her mind was a sieve, admittedly—with a wind blowing through. Son of the commandment? Was this one of those countless Jewish things he had drilled her in, sixteen years ago though it seemed now another lifetime? Well enough she recalled the hours of instruction spent in his airless study, drapes drawn against the heat of the day. It smelled as no vestry ever does. No sweetening telltale of incense there. Only the odor of Gernsbacher's leatherbound out-size volumes, cracked and seamed, which all began on the page where Christian books end. Or did she smell the green velvet bag containing his phylacter-ies? (These were *horrible*. He had taken them out once for her to see, even demonstrated their right use, one little box suspended on the forehead, the other at the left upper arm, adjacent to the heart, and leather straps wound in a prescribed way.) Or was it his prayer shawl she was smelling? Or his creamy homburg, hung up on the door? Some-thing in there didn't smell good.

"Shouldn't we let Felix decide for himself?"

"We certainly should *not!* It's a too serious matter for the boy to appreciate."

But Lucy was already on her feet and crossing the room. She slid open the pocket doors and called upstairs. She put her back against the jamb. She folded her arms. She gave rabbi a look. This was war, he could see, war for the soul of Felix. Hildy sensed it too. She'd come out from behind the lowboy with her tail up in a brush.

Felix clattered down the stairs and came into the parlor. "Felix, you remember Rabbi Gernsbacher, who married your father and me, and blessed this house and" (turning here to rabbi) "christened you."

Gernsbacher shuddered, felt the blush rise under his clothes. Hildy leapt for comfort into the boy's arms, then turned and made the sign of menace at rabbi: her ears flat against her head. Felix held the cat up suddenly right in Gernsbacher's face, and Hildy took a bite of him.

"Oh, rabbi, never try to kiss her when her ears are down!" Lucy cried.

The blood flowed freely from his nose. "I can't stay in this house another minute. I *won't!*" He took a handkerchief from his coat pocket, pressed it to his face. Felix was afraid, for rabbi was fixing to cry, it looked like.

"Just sit yourself down, rabbi—over here, on the chaise. Felix, you take that bad cat out of here! And tell Neevah to hurry up and bring us some iodine and some compresses. We may want salve, too. Now rabbi, just relax. Do you feel faint? Sick to your stomach? Oh, that Hildy can be a villainess. Simply ruled by her moods."

Neevah appeared with the first-aid basket. "Am I supposed to believe what I hear? That our Hildy done bit this man? Tell Neevah what happened."

"Unwind me some gauze, Neevah," Lucy said. This was no ordinary first-aid kit she had brought in but a sizable picnic hamper full of balms, liniments, embrocations, tinctures, Epsoms, purges, and so forth.

From the doorway of the parlor, Hildy draped like a stole around his shoulders, Felix said: "Brace yourself, rabbi, because that tincture of iodine is going to hurt. She's put it on me before—on my knees and elbows but never, I declare, on my nose. I hope it won't hurt *too* bad. I hope you'll be feeling better, rabbi, and that that bite won't get septic . . ."

"Felix, that will *do!*" cried Lucy, whose nerves were raw from all this excitement of rabbi's visit. "Shush him, Neevah." And Neevah held up to Felix the crisscrossed white of her palm. But then brought it back down again on Gernsbacher's weedy shoulder, for rabbi had made to rise from the chaise.

"Keep yuh seat, Mistah Gernsbach."

"Oh, Neevah, you mustn't call him mister," Lucy exhorted, and it was confusing to Neevah, because she'd only intended the highest respect. No Negro man was ever called mister, unless by another Negro. A Negro man could be called reverend or uncle or what have you but not mister. When coloreds were overheard deferring to each other as mister, this was ever a spur to the mirth of white folks. "Call him rabbi, Neevah, same as we do."

CHAPTER SEVEN

A Memory and a Song

RABBI: LITERALLY, MY MASTER. And there were days when Gernsbacher felt masterly. With the early sunshine in his eyes he would say: "This morning am I God's good right arm." But for such a spell of days, as if by an iron law, there came amputation from Him. It was the dreamlike feeling of not being able to flee. There was the wide quietness that was all in all; there was only that. The world was beautiful, yes, but no longer gestured beyond itself. It was just the world; it was no longer Creation; it was uncreated; it was nature. Such thoughts led always to the wisdom of Job's wife: Curse God and die. Tucked into

Scripture, there it had lurked down all the centuries. Way not to be Jewish anymore. Curse God and die.

His teachers at Breslau—Jews in their homes and their synagogues but, in the street, men without the marks of difference, Europeans abreast of European ways, legatees of the great Jewish Enlightenment, exponents to the gentile of the Jew's emergence from backwardness and isolation, practitioners of a dignified rational piety to which no exception could be taken—his teachers at Breslau had noted an unpromising inwardness in young Nathan Gernsbacher, had talked some sense to him about it.

They knew that on certain evenings he betook himself to the bookshop of Hayyim Tarkower—that lunatic, that atavist.

It must be said that Tarkower's was a good store. You could purchase there the necessary, the ennobling texts. But in a backroom at Tarkower's, in a chest under a burden of carpets, were the wayward vicious books by which (such was the Seminary tattle) this strange man led his life. Yes, the *aufgeklärt* rabbis consented to trade with him; he had the best wares in all of Silesia. Passing Tarkower's threshold, however, their noses picked up a drafty fetor, a crosswind from Gehenna.

Each academic year the rabbinate of Breslau could count on it: three or four young seminarians fell under this book vendor's tuition. The backroom of his store served late nights as a *bethhamidrash* for the study of forbidden texts—even, it was rumored, for the offering of forbidden prayers. Here was where you came to learn the thorny theosophical intricacies. Like a candle flickering amid ten mirrors, so the Hidden Infinite bespeaks itself, comes from concealment into manifestation. Tarkower taught them this. Also that the godhead is male and female both, and that the Shekhinah or feminine of God is in exile in the world awaiting reunion with Adonai, her transcendent spouse. Tarkower said God had created the world not in splendor but in catastrophe. Primordial vessels containing emanations of the Hidden Infinite had shattered, he told them, spilling God's light. What was meant to come into existence could not take shape, and the shards of the broken vessels, divine sparks adhering to them, had plunged

down to form this abortion—Tarkower's word—
this abyss of evil, this universe where we live. His
pupils begged to know what is meant by the sepa-
ration of the Shekhinah from her Adonai. She is
the sparks that plunged downward, God among us,
immanent in our deep trouble. Like us she is in
exile; she is in this deep trouble too. Behold the
mother-bird who has strayed from her nest, the
Shekhinah weeping for herself and her chosen.
His pupils entreated how to mend the broken
world. Every individual soul, he told them, in the
course of its wanderings from one life to the next,
must gather the sparks which belong to itself. This
happens through right action, study, and prayer.
When thus we shall have gleaned away from their
immuring shells all the sparks of light, the Messiah
will come forth from hiding. He is at present a beg-
gar somewhere in Rome, Tarkower told his pupils. His body is covered with suppurating sores. He
is seated among the poor lepers. Here is how to
recognize him: whereas the others untie all their
dressings before rebandaging, the Messiah unties
and rebandages each sore separately. Should he be
wanted he must not be delayed.

A Memory and a Song

The faculty at Breslau presented Nathan Gernsbacher with their usual ultimatum—pay attention to rubbish of Tarkower, or pay attention to us. With back in Kalish a mother and three sisters to think of, young Nathan could ill afford to get himself turned out of seminary. He came to heel, conceded the error of his ways. Several others were made to do so as well. The rabbis spelled out rugged probationary terms. An early supper, gentlemen, and to your rooms. They had by now some large experience of this camel's nose under the tent, knew how to scotch it. Farewell to hole-and-corner catechizings, deliberative late walks home, drifted snow wastes through which, unfearing, a seeker for truth, one followed the hidden crook and bend. Tarkower, farewell . . .

But that magus, that thaumaturge, that gnostic in pince-nez was omnipresent. Really, it was remarkable to go out and not to collide with him. "A day made of diamonds," he would note if it was fair, and eloquently doff his hat. He was graciousness itself, treated everyone the same. On went the smile and off came the hat whether he knew you or not.

Something, meanwhile, was giving way in Nathan. He cast about for the right word. It was: purpose. "My purpose is breaking." He ruminated on what his mother in Kalish, as full of notions as is a pomegranate of seeds, had used to say when he was small. "If there are *mazikim* lurking, they will catch our prayers and keep them from going up to God; this is what evil spirits want to do; they want to steal our prayers." It had come swift to him that his mother's kitchen wisdom and the darkly radiant theurgy of Tarkower were really one and the same. And for what, if not for these, could he feel love? Scoured of the bogeys, the revenants, the souls in transit from one incarnation to the next, cleansed of all madness, made seemly for the gentile inspection, what was Judaism? "A fossil," Nathan murmured. "I am tending a fossil."

Tend it he did. He was brilliant among his classmates in the historical study of Mishnah, Gemara, and Midrash. On Yom Kippur he put on a gold-threaded kittel and led the Neilah—an extreme honor for one so recently in disgrace, but the rabbis were well pleased with their reconstructed Gernsbacher and wished to distinguish him. They did

not know that a dread advocacy had begun to
sound in Nathan's brain. Sometimes loud, sometimes barely audible; but unyielding. Fellows at the
rooming house where he rented would hear thud-
ding in the night—Gernsbacher's head against the
bedpost. Like an appointed lot, a portion, a cup,
Job's wife was not to be evaded.

It was the week of Simchath Torah before Nathan dared again to enter Tarkower's. The familiar
thrumming had by then settled down at the base of
his skull. He'd contrived a way to live with it. Not
since Shavuoth had he banged his head in the
night. Because he heard Job's wife absolutely all
the time, he mostly no longer heard her. On this
particular day in autumn he had gone in search of
The Sermons of the Jews by Leopold Zunz.

"Ach, a fine work," Tarkower declared, smiling
blandly. He turned and bustled up a ladder to fetch
the volume. "Yes, yes, the great Zunz. Formidable
mind. Absolutely *gründlich* for your training, my
boy."

"Do you remember me, Mr. Tarkower?"

"Remember you? I remember all of you fine
boys. Thirty years of seminarians, and I remember

every one." Down he came, smiling still, blowing dust from the binding of Zunz's masterwork. "Hayyim Tarkower never forgets a boy." His pince-nez in their steel frame gave back the light.

"You'll pardon my saying, sir, that in this case you *don't* really seem to remember. I'm Gernsbacher. I'm one of the students who used to come here in the evenings last winter—"

At this, Tarkower spread wide his hands. He shook his head. Exhortingly, the pince-nez flashed at Nathan.

"—to study—"

Tarkower shook his head.

"—the hidden books."

Tarkower removed the pince-nez. Only now could Nathan see the unshed tears in his eyes. "I implore you, young man, not to speak of that . . . Forget about it . . . Forget about it for a long, long time . . . Pay attention to the rabbis, God preserve them. It's the rabbis who will point the way to your future. A pulpit, a congregation, no? Circumcisions, marriages, funerals.

"Need I say that you must find yourself a fine girl?" he went on quickly. "That's essential. A bach-

elor rabbi? A shame, that would be. No one listens
to bachelors—their words are a chaff the wind
blows away. Forget the aberrations of last winter,
my boy. Forget what you heard here. Maunderings
of an old charlatan who's not known how to honor
God's commandment with his body, much less his
mind. What wisdom can there be, I ask you, from a
wifeless, childless man—a *bachelor?*" This word he
spat out like a rancid mouthful. "Forget what you
heard here . . ."

Without explanation Tarkower fled to the backroom. Nathan could hear an ecstatic mumble, but
not make out the words; the familiar creak of the
trunk being opened; a moment or two of rummag-
ing. Then he heard the lid slam shut.

Tarkower reappeared. In both hands he was
clutching a little book in green leather. His face
burned like a torch. "Until you will be more than
seventy! Seventy, do you hear?" His German had
quite failed him; he was shouting now in *mamaloshen.* "Then—cut these pages, read these words!
When you will be more than seventy, and not a day
before. Do you swear it?"

"I—I don't think I can swear—"

"Swear it, young man!"

"I—"

"Swear it!"

"I swear, Mr. Tarkower." A chill of fever had started up Nathan's back. Tarkower held forth the little book. In dread Nathan reached out, hastily confiding it to his coat pocket. It was as if a charge had thus been lifted from the old man and placed upon the young one. Tarkower was suddenly pacific. The blaze went from him. Reassuming his former amenity, he again became a salesman. "Now let me see . . ." The Zunz was a very luxurious book; it had gold leaf on the spine and marbled end papers. After reflection Tarkower quoted a price, not too dear yet not a steal. He was all retailer now. The terrible kabbalist of a minute ago—admonishing, inspired—had vanished. "Peace to you, my boy."

"And to you, sir," Nathan managed to say. His mouth tasted sour and hot. He was getting sick, he knew it. He hastened back to the rooming house, feeling his bowels turn to water as he went.

Next day Nathan was absent from all classes of instruction, as well as from the morning and evening devotions. High temperature and a fulminating diarrhoea confined him to his room. The little book in green leather lay with him under his blankets. He had noticed that it gave off a warming radiance, so he slipped it into his nightshirt.

Friends looking in on him evinced concern for Nathan's recovery. To stave off pneumonia they suggested a mustard bath. But Nathan needed no mustard bath, not with his book to protect him.

Late that evening the fever spiked. A voice in the room said, "Fear nothing." But whether it came from his own throat or from the book Nathan could not tell. "Cut me, read me." Yes, then; it *was* the book.

Nathan said: "I am sworn in a vow to wait for my old age."

The book replied: "Old age? If this fever worsens, you'll not see tomorrow morning. Cut me, read me!"

Nathan had heard it said—God ministers with voices to those who are dying alone. Absolute abandonment in that hour He will not permit.

"Then I must be dying."

But the book cried out: "Nathan, Nathan, I am

no usher of death. Nathan, I am your life. Cut me, read me!" And the room swam wickedly before his eyes.

Nathan's candle was by that hour down to the socket. He summoned energy to light a fresh one, hands shaking pitifully, then took a letter knife from his bedside table, cut at random a page of the little book. The words were hard to make out, as if under a veil. Hebrew flickered on the upper half of the page, Yiddish underneath. The text was a story, he saw. It was entitled "The Wise Man and the Simpleton" and went as follows:

> *Two men received identical messages from the king. One of these men was considered wise; the other was known as a simpleton. Whereas the so-called simpleton responded quickly to the king, and so received his due reward, the 'wise' man said to the sage who had brought his letter: 'Wait here tonight and let us discuss this matter' . . . The wise man, with his philosophic mind, set to thinking about it and said: 'Why should the king be sending for an unimportant fellow like me? Who am I that the king, out of all his vast kingdom, should send for me? Compared to the king I am*

nobody; how can it possibly make sense that the king should send someone after a person as small as I am? If I were to say that it is because of my wisdom—certainly the king has his own sages, and he himself is also a very wise man. So what is this matter of the king's sending for me?' He became very much confounded by it until finally he said: 'It is now very clear in my mind that there is no king in the world at all. The world is full of fools who think there is a king. How is it possible that they should all have subjected themselves to one man, thinking that he is the king, when in reality there is no king at all?'

The messenger answered him: 'But I brought you a message from the king!' The wise man asked: 'Did you receive that message from the king's own hand?' The messenger was obliged to admit that he had not, but rather that someone else had given him the message in the king's name. The wise man continued: 'See how right I am—there is no king at all!' He said to the messenger: 'You have lived all your life in the capital. Tell me, have you ever seen the king?' The messenger replied that he had not. (This is indeed the case. Not everyone merits to see the king, who reveals himself only on very rare occasions.) And the wise man responded: 'Now see how indubitably my position has been proven; there is no king at all, for even you have not seen him.' So the two of them decided that the king did not exist. They went into the market and there they came upon a soldier. 'Whom do you serve?' they asked him. 'The king,' he replied. 'Have you ever seen this king?' 'No.' 'What a fool,' they thought . . .

Sweat rushed from Nathan in a torrent as he read the tale. Then his body ceased its roiling. The little volume slipped from his hand. The candle flame, a sentinel, stood straight up. Nathan slept the blithe unbothered sleep of youth.

Aw, that nose'll be fine," Neevah tossed over her shoulder as she left the room, not sparing the note of contempt. She shut the pocket doors behind her. "Little old scratch on his nose!" It was really too much, a grown-up and grown-old man carrying on thus. "Mistah Gernsbach think he's pretty!" Her laughter came in a single high note, derisive as a catbird's.

And where was the unabject individual who had raised such a roughhouse? In Felix's room, washing her paws. Now she cocked an ear. Muffled sounds of music were coming upstairs from the parlor.

Felix felt, with due respect, that the caller downstairs had outstayed his welcome. It would be suppertime directly. There had been silence for a little while from the parlor, now there was music. Felix came downstairs and opened the pocket doors for just a peek. Rabbi was supine—napping, it looked like. The bandaged nose stuck up from under a handkerchief Lucy had spread across his face.

She was seated at the piano, her back to the door. She was playing, with the soft pedal, something of Lehár she'd learned. A New Orleans sheet-music vendor who sent on approval the latest songs and operettas, a very nice man by his letters, had most recently commended to Lucy *Die lustige Witwe*.

It has been the toast of Vienna, and now of London, too, dear Mrs. Mehmel. I am presuming to send you the original German lyrics, as you have expressed this preference. I trust you will not consider me impertinent to offer for your consideration a song book with this title. You wrote to us that you are a widow. Believe me that my lovely wife and I were grieved to learn this. But we can only conclude by the vivacity and charm of your letters that you are not one to be bowed down by life's hammer blows. My beloved Arlette joins me in wishing you all the pleasure—and, yes, *merriment!*—that sheet music can bring to a home. In closing, dear Mrs. Mehmel, let it not come amiss if I remind you of an outstanding obligation of four dollars and eighty-seven cents against your account. This is doubtless an oversight, but the arrearage has stood on our books for some months now. We are confident that you will want to satisfy it in a timely manner. Your obedient servant.

What Lucy played was a beautiful song about a sprite—a Vilja—seen by a hunter one day in a glen.

Es lebt' eine Vilja, ein Waldmaegdelein,
ein Jaeger erschaut' sie im Felsengestein!

Under Lucy's handkerchief, Gernsbacher hearkened to the words and music. He wasn't really napping. He was possuming. He was lying there thinking with shame of how he'd paid this call to expostulate with Lucy and how she, the boy, the colored woman, the cat—the whole irregular household—had vanquished him. "Something happened, God forbid, to your nose?" the rebbitsin would ask when he got home, and then he'd have to tell her.

Das Walmaegdelein strecte die hand nach ihm aus
Und zog ihn hinein in ihr folsiges Haus.

Frau Gernsbacher would put questions. Had the wound been properly cleaned? Was there not some danger of lockjaw, or rabies? Why was the Mehmels' cat not muzzled? Should such a menace be allowed to live?

Rivka Gernsbacher had plighted her troth to rabbi in the humblest way. Yes: she had been a mail-order bride. A girl from Brody, in the part of Poland under Austro-Hungarian administration, moderately good-looking (or at least representable as such in a daguerreotype) but with no dowry, she found her benefit in a willingness to travel purblindly and travel far. When the marriage broker showed a rotogravure of the young rabbi in front of a studio curtain—palms clashing in the wind, combers breaking—and read to her a description of the demi-heaven in which this suitor lived, it sufficed. She posted to Texas a letter accepting his offer of marriage. She made her way to Hamburg and, with funds Nathan had forwarded, got on a boat. She wanted a first-hand look at those palm trees, those waves.

Nothing had turned out right. Rivka wrote bitter letters home to her kinfolk, describing Galveston as a wicked jest life had played. Oh, very pretty, yes, but uninhabitable, laid over with a curse. Anywhere else and marriage would have given her arms a child to hold. Not here. Here she had only an evil itch in the eyes. And obstreperous gastric troubles, clay-colored stools. Also vaguer complaints: a pain that circulated freely, sometimes declaring itself in her extremities, sometimes in her chest, sometimes in her blighted womb. "Galveston has done this to me, Nathan Gernsbacher. Do you hear? Listen when I'm talking to you. I'm talking to you, Nathan . . ."

A Memory and a Song

Vilja, o Vilja, Du Waldmaegdelein,
fass' mich und lass' mich dein Trautliebster sein!

Rabbi played his wife no attention. Long since, her voluble misery had ceased to register on him. Not a well woman? She'd bury us all and complain for her own sake.

Vilja, o Vilja, was tust Du mir an?
Bang fleht ein liebkranker Mann!

Lucy's musical entertainment was now at an end. Rabbi drew her handkerchief from his face and sat up. His nose hurt. Standing over him was Neevah, who'd taken a bold initiative to bring this interview to term. She had brought rabbi's hat into the parlor, and turned it now this way and that, as if the homburg were perhaps a for-the-nonce aberration of nature, or perhaps a precious relic of some lost civilization, or perhaps a conclusive piece of evidence against Nathan Gernsbacher, the accused.

"I will be going along now," he said.

Neevah handed rabbi his hat. Lucy bade him goodbye and thanked him for his visit, the purpose of which lay buried now under silt and rubble of that afternoon.

"Goodbye, rabbi!" Felix called from his bedroom window. "You have a nice evening, rabbi!" He fished about for something else polite to holler at the clenched figure disappearing down Broadway. "Happy days, rabbi!" Hildy, beside the boy, put on a private smile. A wavelet rode the fur along her back. She shut her topaz eyes and slept.

CHAPTER EIGHT

Who Goes There?

RICH, OTIOSE, SUMMER fooled along. Into that torpor came a stranger walking. Schmulowicz was his name. Old, old, wind-burned and old. Wore a moose-colored duster in despite of the heat. Shoes were a lumpy pair of brogues, down-at-heel, hobnailed, somebody else's before. Kept his trousers in place by means of a string.

Old? He was older than old. With a neck as skinny as a cart shaft; and bug-eyes, signifying pathos; and nowhere the trace of a smile.

"Who *are* you, mister?" Felix asked at the corner

of Post Office and Twelfth. He in particular, and Galveston in general, were interested to know.

The ancient of days said nothing, unbuckling his grip instead and taking from it a little board furnished with the letters of the alphabet. S-c-h-m-u-l-o-w-i-c-z, he spelled, pointing to each letter in turn. I—a-m—S-c-h-m-u-l-o-w-i-c-z. "How do," said Felix. There they stood awhile, getting acquainted in the shade of the Baptist steeple. "You need refreshment, mister." Felix took the stranger's spidery hand in his own and led him in the direction of the Sugar Bush, an alehouse at the corner of Market and Eighteenth. Together along sidewalks concentrating the heat they walked, Felix surefooted, Schmulowicz stumbling as in blindman's bluff. For while his mind was distance, the pure lure of distance, his body was but sticks and staves barely sufficing to uphold him.

"Galveston's pretty, isn't it?" Felix said.

When the stranger lifted his barren eyebrows, this meant yes.

"You been this way before?"

For no, the lower lip protruded.

Who Goes There?

At Sugar Bush the barkeep recommended a delicious drink, a schnapps made with juniper. Schmulowicz turned his eyes upwards in delight and drank the ardent spirits down.

All eyes, of course, had turned to take the stranger's measure. The barkeep for his part had gone sullen because Schmulowicz was answering the customary small talk with only a Bedouin-like stare. What's your name? Where you from? Only the black splendor of his eyes answered, shards from a burnt-out star. What's your line? Where you been? Cat got your tongue, fella? A customer, a regular of the place, a man of what Miss Murph would call "rural mien," stepped up to say (and forcibly this time): "Where you from?" The barkeep went about his business, slicing the froth off of beer mugs with a deal paddle. Variable weather at Sugar Bush, Felix perceived. He sought to recover the unclouded horizon of a few moments before by explaining: "He's mute."

"But can he hear us, son?" asked a second man who had got to this feet.

"Yes sir, I do believe he can." And then Felix

added, at a venture: "He's from no place around here. He's from overseas, don't you know." At this the stranger's eyebrows rose in a slow majesty. He produced the alphabet board and spelled G-r-o-d-n-o—G-u-b-e-r-n-y-a. Nothing; no response from anyone there. Never heard of the place. A man at one end of the bar began to play mournfully his drag harmonica.

The stranger tried again. R-u-s-s-i-a, he spelled. Now a susurrus of recognition and pleasure passed through the room. Bitsie Moss, the waitress at Sugar Bush, a hapless woman with heavy eyeglasses and a gap-toothed face, who was the object of pitiless japes from the menfolk which she was meant to overhear, for these were not gentlemen, observed that whereas the United States is in the middle of the world map Russia is split in two and shoved over to either side. Bitsie wanted to know, was Russia two places or one? The man of rural mien hushed her with a snort and a guffaw.

"Oh, more than two," Felix said, and the man of rural mien, abashed now, peered down into his tumbler of beer. Felix continued: "Russia includes what were formerly Poland and Lithuania. Also

Latvia and Estonia. Also Georgia, Bylorussia and the Ukraine." He went to the window pane, filthy from the inside with smoke, and drew the outline of great Mother Russia. Easy for him; he could draw any country you cared to name and fill in the important cities, mountain ranges, bodies of water. Now he indicated where the Volga flows. And the Ob, the Yenisei, the Lena, and the Kolyma. He showed them Sakhalin Island and the Sea of Okhotsk. He showed the Bering Strait, the East Siberian Sea, along with all the other seas hedging Russia about—the Laptev, the Kara, the Barents, the Baltic, the Black, the Caspian. He showed them where the Tundra is, and where the Taiga. He showed Mount Elbrus. He indicated where are Saint Petersburg and Moscow, the two citadels of Muscovy. And there were the arcane towns to mention: Talinn, Riga, Lvov, Minsk, Sevastopol, Tbilisi, Samarkand, places that to say the names of is like breathing some rare ether.

But what a learning-loving boy of fourteen has to say about the world is of no interest in a barrel house. Except for Bitsie everyone in Sugar Bush had promptly ceased to listen. Felix didn't care.

With the emphasis due, he now indicated Grodno on his improvised map. The stranger clapped hands together in delight, asseverated wildly with his brow.

Roache and Munger were having a couple of beers in one corner of the place. Roache called out for another round: "Two more Sweet Brooks, if you please, barkeep!"

The man of rural mien looked up gravely from his table one over from theirs. "You *drink* that hog piss?" he asked.

"These days we do, yep. Drink it down as best we can on account of a little financial arrangement me and Pete here got with the brewers. Worst damn beer there is!"

Thus to hear the family concern exposed to slighting reference didn't sit right with Felix. Was not Sweet Brook the most delicious beverage on earth? The most delicious, surely. He paid the barkeep, gathered up the stranger and they took their leave.

Bitsie Moss stared and stared after them. She set down a tray of tumblers and stepped out the front door, adjusting her eyeglasses for another look.

Who Goes There?

"Bitsie, you lummox!" her employer was saying when she came back in.

The sun at its zenith was blinding. Beneath it Felix and Schmulowicz made their way along sidewalks buckling with the heat they held.

"You tired, mister?"

The stranger allowed as he was tired. He had everyone in shoe leather staring at him; enough to wear a body down. Along the Strand were hunched together various blowhards who turned now, leaving off with their lies. Also, and immemorially, there was a wet-eyed mulatta who cut silhouettes for two bits apiece, and sold spool thread, in addition, and buttons and safety pins. But it was her silhouettes that were a tradition of the place. People obtained them over and over again from her, who had passed beyond youth into middle age and now beyond middle age into her decline, occupying the same corner, vending the same wares. ("Velma Truley's profile has not changed an iota in these thirty *years!*" Murph liked to boast among friends, and Miss Truley would say, "Oh, silliness, Etta Mae," but Murph would go and take down from the wall the chronology of Truley's profile, eight or ten silhouetted images, black cloth paper pasted onto white, set cameo-style and displayed in a burl wood frame, to prove that it was so . . .)

"I'll go first," Felix said, for the stranger was balking, as if the taking of one's silhouette were a pilfering of the soul. Felix sat himself down and turned one side to her. He canted his lips and made goosegog eyes, thinking this would lend dignity. *"No hagas eso,"* the silhouettest said, neither irritated nor amused, studying him with one eye closed, wheezing and muttering, plying quickly her scissors. Done, she brushed the image with paste and laid it on a white background, then took twenty-five cents from the boy.

Now it was the stranger's turn. Reluctant still, but resigned, he removed his heavy limp-collared duster and handed it to Felix. From Schmulowicz's open shirt the breastbone stood out sharply, same as a bird's, Felix saw. Schmulowicz seated himself in front of the silhouettist, lifted his olden head to the breeze.

The mulatta closed one eye, inclined speculatively her head of ginger hair mixed with gray. Her scissors commenced suddenly; then suddenly they stopped, deadlocked by what she saw. Her rheumy eyes flashed, her mouth tightened. "*Hay demasiadas caras aquí!*" she cried in exasperation, in defeat. Too many faces. It was true. Too many faces in Schmulowicz's face. You saw there, by turns, scarecrow age and indomitable youth. "*Hay demasiadas caras aquí,*" the mulatta said again, softly this time, with awe.

Who was this unclassifiable person? Felix found himself palpating eight or ten peculiar rounded lumps under the buckram lining of the overcoat and wondered what they could be. What forbidden thing was the stranger conveying?

Then again it happened. Without warning Schmulowicz the stranger changed himself before their eyes from sticks and staves into the rutilant flower of youth.

The mulatta drew in her breath sharply. She covered her mouth with one hand, pointed a squabby finger at Schmulowicz with the other. Here was a business she had thought only sleeping earth could transact, new life out of old. She did not make the cross sign; she clean forgot about Father, Son, and Holy Spirit abiding and her thought was all of earth, of its rugged marvels.

"*El tiempo va y viene*," she murmured to herself. Felix caught the gist of it.

So did Schmulowicz. "T-i-m-e—g-o-e-s—t-o—a-n-d—f-r-o," he averred with pleasure on his board.

"W-h-e-r-e-v-e-r—y-o-u—l-o-o-k—t-w-i-c-e—w-h-e-r-e-v-e-r—y-o-u—l-o-o-k—t-w-i-c-e—t-i-m-e—b-o-t-h—w-a-y-s—i-s—h-u-r-r-y-i-n-g."

Then, in the instant, Schmulowicz was old again.

CHAPTER NINE

Traveler, Halt!

VELMA TRULEY would remember to the end of her days what she had been doing when Felix brought the stranger to Winnie Street. She had been shelling purple-hulled peas on the front step and she had been remonstrating with Bob.

Here is why:

The previous morning a farmer from the westerly end of the island had brought several of his swine to town for slaughter. It was a longish trip and a hottish day and the plank bench of the wain was hard and the farmer had accordingly resolved to keep himself company with a bottle of home wine—held for a while between his feet, then for a while to his lips, and so on. He had not meant to go past moderation, but the tannic savor of the wine was a refreshment from the gathering heat of day, a comfort against vagaries awaiting him in town. Unawares, he relinquished his sobriety.

What happened a moment or two after he had tied up to a snubbing post at the corner of Mechanic and Twenty-fourth is unclear, but someone, just a mischievous person, or perhaps an enemy, must have lifted the hasp of the tailgate of this farmer's wain, permitting the livestock to make their escape. Hogs fanned out every which way, doing destruction as they went. A shoat pig, quicker than the rest, came pell-mell up Winnie Street, shot through Truley's four-o'clocks and made for the back yard. It was here that Bob, in high dudgeon and out of his mind with delight, brought the shoat to bay along a derelict fence grown over with hop vine and verbena. Truley and Murph bounded from the back door. Truley reached for the bellowing dog and Murph for the shrilling pig . . .

"Might have killed the little thing," Miss Truley

said now, not looking up from her apron near full of shelled peas. "Bad boy; *very* bad!" But all she really meant by her dispraise was: *I love you so much, you big brute, I can't hardly stand it.* She let the mask of censure fall, said:

"Come here, handsome. Try one of these. Don't care for it?"

No response, because Bob was just then unwilling to be talked to as a dog. He stared over his shoulder, then back at Truley. This is important—*important!*—said the yellow eyes. Bob did not whine or bark. He put his curtailed tail level with the horizon and looked dead on at Truley.

The front gate creaked low and pitiful-sounding when Felix put his hand to it and its picket shadows lengthened up the little footpath to where Truley sat. She was staring hard at her dog, Felix observed, and he at her. What on earth?

"Miss Truley? Miss Truley?"

"Why, Felix honey, to what do we owe—" Here she broke off, having clapped eyes on the boy's extraordinary companion.

Bringing him here was an uncertain gambit, to be sure. But the doormat said "Welcome" to all and sundry. Felix was taking the ladies at their word.

"Miss Truley, can he live here?" the boy asked.

"Come again."

"I say, can he live here." In Winnie Street it was best coming straight to the point, he knew.

Truley put one hand up for a sun visor and looked the stranger over slow. "Etta Mae," she called out at length. Miss Murph appeared behind the screen of the upstairs window. "Etta Mae, I expect you'd better come down here."

Murph had not been feeling well that day. Too much of cantaloupe at the noon meal had given her a flux. Truley played doctor to the complaint, prescribing Pat-a-cake biscuits smeared with curd, a known specific against loose bowels. It had worked like a charm. Better now, Murph paused in front of the chiffonier; added a couple of steel combs to the back of her hairdo; re-pinned the watch to her overblouse. Then she turned to smooth out the counterpane stitched in candlewicking and to pat up the pillows where earlier she had laid her sick head.

Stairboards creaking steadfastly beneath her,

here she came now: in aspect discouraging, pale-
ish yellow, the color of something grown under-
ground, for she was an indoors woman, did not
require the light. The front screen slapped to
behind her. "Etta Murph," she said, coming down
the front step, her hand up to greet the shapeless
dingy mass beside Felix.

The stranger said nothing (of course) but took
the alphabet board from the side pocket of his grip
and started in. Murph let the unclasped hand fall
to her side.

"I—a—m—S-c-h-m-u-l-o-w-i-c-z."

"He's Schmulowicz," Felix iterated, but Murph
put the boy to silence with a wave of her hand.

Fastened now on the stranger, she blinked hard,
tried to blink away this strangeness. "We are
pleased to meet you," she said at last, whereupon
Miss Truley turned her eyes very high, stood up
holding the corners of her apron so as not to spill
the little harvest of peas and said:

"If you don't mind, Etta Murph, I would like to
have a word with you, in the *kitchen!*"

Murph held the front screen for her, then closed
the kitchen door when they got there, crossed her

short arms across her barrel and said, "What?" A many-tined stag's head, objectionable to Truley but admired by Murph, stared down temperately upon them both.

Truley had shaken the hulled peas out of her apron into a colander. She continued in a low voice: "You ought to get your head out of the clouds, missy. You ought to read some news. We got us a passel of strange folks come to town, I saw by the papers this morning. Jews, they are, from Russia." She reached for that afternoon's Galveston *Intelligencer*, unfolded it with drama, took a seat and began to read aloud from page one.

> We are no strangers to the immigrant. Our fair port has stood witness to the downtrodden but hopeful, arriving from the four corners, yearning to breathe free. Yesterday morning sixty-six men, six women, and fifteen children, former subjects of the Russian Tsar, all of them members of the Jewish race, debarked from the *S.S. Cassel*, a familiar ship in port here, bound from Bremen, Germany. They are in Galveston only long enough to receive occupational assignments to points north. Two carpenters, a tailor, and a lens grinder will take up res-

idence in Little Rock, where their new employers
eagerly await them. Likewise the joiner and the
three blacksmiths—

Here Truley broke off. Was Etta not listening?
Was Etta in one of her absentations, moods of non-
attendance? Had Etta taken her usual French
leave? Mostly Murph's eyes were a greenish brown,
same as many other people's. But sometimes, and
now was one of them, the color would drain away
and what was left looked like—it was hard to
describe—like scratched quartz with the sunlight
filtering through. Those frightful orbs would have
undone a lesser woman than Truley. Thirty years
ago she had looked into them and been afraid. In
time, though, she was consoled to grasp that a
Cumaen Sibyl when thinking hard can't help it, just
looks that way. There had anyhow been things
tougher to deal with than those eyes. Don't kid
yourself: life with the Sibyl is no fandango. "Pay
attention, you!" enjoined Truley, then went on with
her reading.

—Likewise the joiner and the three blacksmiths
who go to Saint Louis; the cobbler who is bound for

Council Bluffs; the stone mason going to Tulsa; the glazier and the bookbinder on his way to Sioux Falls; and the two bakers and the egg candler who will reside in Milwaukee. Others are to be settled in some of the smaller towns of Louisiana and East Texas including—Bossier City, Opelousas, and Shreveport; Waxahachie, Corsicana, Tyler, and Nacogdoches. Rabbi Nathan Gernsbacher, who was down to the dockyard to greet his newly arrived coreligionists, explained that some of them are expected by relatives who have already arrived: a mother and her two children, for example, will soon be reunited with her husband and their father, an upholsterer working in Denver these last eighteen months. Others have come ahead to earn money that will pay the westward passage of loved ones still in Russia. Mayor Critchmar of our fair city offered the immigrants words of welcome, with Rabbi Gernsbacher acting as translator into their Jewish language: "You have come to a great country," the mayor told them. "With industry and economy all of you will meet with success. Obey the laws and try to make good citizens." A spokesman for the new arrivals, a former schoolteacher from the Ukraine, which is a southern region of Russia, answered Mayor Critchmar as follows: "We are overwhelmed that the ruler of the city should greet us. We have never been spoken to by the officials of our country except in terms of harshness, and although we have heard of the great land of freedom, it is very hard to realize that we are permitted to grasp the hand of the great man." The young teacher added in conclusion, "We will do everything we can to make good citizens." All of Galveston joins the Intelligencer, we are certain, in wishing these brave pilgrims good luck and Godspeed!

Miss Truley shot Murph a trenchant glance over the half-lens spectacles she nowadays wore for close work and kept on a ribbon around her neck. She licked her index finger, leafed noisily to a small box near the bottom of page eleven. "Concernment Mounts," she reported, quoting the little headline. She read on:

As we go to press, the Bureau of Immigration is voicing worry over the whereabouts of one of the eighty-seven Hebrews of Russian origin who were disembarked yesterday from *S.S. Cassel*. A discrepancy between official tallies and the ship's manifest has led to different speculations, direst of which is that some Jew fell overboard upon the high seas. The Intelligencer will have more as details come to light.

Truley folded the paper and laid it crosswise in her lap. "Etta Mae, that's him."

Murph didn't pay her any attention. Murph was in the mind now, Murph was at the windy crossroads. The world blew through her. Snow mountains, for example. And waste gray oceans where there is no land to see. And the smaller things, like empires. And smaller still, persons, who are but the driftage of history. "*Siste, viator*," she murmured after lengthy silence. Traveler, halt.

Murph settled onto a rush-bottom chair, took the shagreen tobacco pouch from her shirtwaist pocket, commenced to roll a smoke. She lit up, strained the first long suction through her teeth. Lolling her head backwards, staring half-absent at the tin-press ceiling, she exhaled the smoke in rings that caught and broke up one another. Oh, it would have been easy enough—wouldn't it?—telling Schmulowicz to take his flea-bitten life somewhere else. He had no money? He had better get some. He had no prospects? It was surely not their problem. But Felix's queer frankhearted question, carried indoors with them—*Can he live here?*—expanded in the mind.

Traveler, Halt!

"Live *here*?" Truley had been stung to say. "Did you *smell* of him? *Did* you?" She had a point, for the odor off of Schmulowicz—recondite, pervasive— was of the way little boys acridly reek after playing hard, and of the mingled smell of men with women, and of the frowsty smell of oldsters who are bedridden and not going to get well, and of the outright stench of carrion. Schmulowicz stank of life and death.

Her gaze still fixed to the ceiling, Murph mooted an idea to Truley: "We could let him the boathouse . . . Really, we could *give* it to him for a while, couldn't we?" She herself never went there. It was Truley's, in practice as in title, her father having set the parcel and the house over to her in his will. Abutting the easterly reach of Offatts Bayou, it had been her delight and solace, for Truley was a superb fisherwoman, would spend whole days casting from the bank or from a cedar-ribbed pirogue on the property which she would row out and put to anchor in the brackish laze of the bayou.

With this pirogue went a terrible story. Years past, an uncle of hers, a Mr. Orvis Truley, her father's youngest brother, had greatly shocked

Galveston. Miss Truley was only a little girl at the time, but ahead of everybody she understood what had happened and what it meant. Orvis was an ungainly and imbecile fellow who they said had never had a woman his whole life long. He was able to hold down only menial jobs offered him on sufferance by family members. What mind he had Orvis could not keep on his work. Leaving chores half-done he would skulk off to somewhere private, kick out of his shoes and socks and coverall and underclothes and indulge a lonely vice more appropriate to youth than to manhood. Poor onanist, he preferred his exploits in the out of doors, partly for the feel of the weather on his body, partly for the increased risk of getting caught . . . As, of course, he eventually did.

Galveston Island boasted of many beautiful ladies, and Orvis in his solitude possessed them all. Roughly he would call their names, commanding each what to do for his further pleasure. Then, at the crisis, he would blurt out his true heart's longing, who were colored twin girls, Wanell and Gyrene Milfus, daughters of a stable hand, whom Orvis would observe each Sunday striding arm in arm to church, dressed up beautiful along with their many brothers and sisters, like cygnets in the wake of the estimable God-fearing hostler and his wife. Orvis had first caught sight of them one Sunday morning on a stroll through Nigger Town. Afterwards he discovered, to his confoundment, that by that one look their way he'd been whelmed. The pretty faces of Wanell and Gyrene grew bright in Orvis Truley's hebetudinous mind. Their girlish splendor dogged him, try as he might to train himself on other, seemlier lusts: the marriageable daughter of a wealthy local tungsten processor, the child bride of an apothecary-surgeon newly arrived in town, the draggletail known to habituate railroad yards after dark. Once, in his desperation, he made love to a sassafras tree, wrapping his naked arms and legs around the skinny trunk, crying, "Sassafras, sassafras," till he was played out. But when the grimace went from his mouth and he unclenched his eyes, it was Wanell and Gyrene Milfus who were there to wipe his drenched brow and bestow kisses everywhere on his spent person.

What was bound to happen, happened. Orvis got caught. Lackamercy on him, the jokes knew no end. Women speculated in whispers on this case of self-abuse, and buried hot faces in their hands. Men roared about it and poked each other in the ribs. Strumming the banjo, they called it. Orvis had been found in broad daylight, bare as the good Lord made him, strum-ming on the old ban-jo. You observed in the street grown men behaving with the cruelty of boys, turning from Orvis with bleak smiles, singing, "Fee-fie-fiddli-ai-o, fee-fie-fiddli-ai-o," like that, and winking at one another.

The object of such wholesome fun is meant to take it in good part. This is a postulate of the school yard, familiar from earliest youth, which the victim is meant to understand and to concur in. This is the way of the world. His pain is but the sidelight in a larger scheme of diversion, laughter, fun. We are only joking, we mean no harm. This ninny is not meant to call aloud to high heaven for justice. When he does, when his cry is so desolating that our pleasure gets spoiled and our laughter ceases, we feel that the victim has badly let us down.

Orvis placed two identical bouquets on the door-step of the peeling frame house of a certain Negro hostler. The bouquets were composed of sneeze-weed and mullein, harebell and blue vervain and were bound together with washline. Orvis then went to the boathouse his brother owned on Offatts Bayou and dragged a pirogue from the shed down to the bank. He pushed off for deep water. When he got there he backpaddled a moment, then took a knife and spool of washline from his pocket. He sat very still for a long time. Then he took hold of the gunwales and, rocking the canoe briskly side to side, made the shiftless water spank beneath the hull. Across the surface, shocks went forth. Orvis sat very still again. He watched the circles widening, flattening. He cut two lengths of washline, laid one across the gunwale and with the other tied his left foot to the stern thwart. He sat still a while more. Then, as if to some experimental end, he tied the other foot. Then he cut two more lengths of cord, lay down with his back to the ribs and planks and his face to the sky and tied his left wrist to the bow thwart. Using his teeth he managed to fasten similarly the right wrist.

Then he flipped the pirogue over.

Have you heard about that desperate youth in

Chicago who attempted to throw his life away? Like a plummet he went from the roof of the newly completed Schlesinger & Meyer Store, corner of State and Madison. As chance would have it, though, a lorry of loose hay was passing below just then to catch him, easeful as a feather bed. It is a famous story. Afterwards, when reporters beset the youth to learn what his thoughts had been as he dropped, he said he'd utterly repented as soon as he was in the air. Had he known the merciful lorry was beneath him as he fell? No, no, for he had looked straight up while on his way down . . .

Almost at once, in the darkness of the upturned pirogue, Orvis's wrists and ankles were bleeding, rubbed raw in the panic sudden fear. Arching himself so that his mouth and nose were just out of the water, he screamed. This went on for some time. At first he was penitential, beseeching: "Jesus! Sweet *Je-sus—help ME!*" But in due course his drowning mouth did utter every conceivable blasphemy.

Two passersby, virtuous young men coming up the towpath, could just make out, muffled but urgent, the name of their Lord being cried. From whence? Oh, sakes alive, from that upturned piro-gue out on the bayou! They yanked their shoes off and dove in to save whoever was under there. When they reached the canoe and righted it they said, "Orvis, you poor bastard!" and asked, "Who did this wicked thing?" Somebody had gone too far. "Who did it, Orvis?"

But he would not say. Galveston had given him the high hat; now he was returning the favor. From that day, townspeople were accountably eager not to add to his injury. "Morning, Orvis!" . . . "Top of the day to you, Orvis!" . . . "Why, Orvis, that crush hat is most becoming!" . . . "Orvis, we thought you might enjoy some of this devil's food cake old Mrs. Diligdisch has prepared!" . . . "Care for a cigar, Orvis? Finest Cuban leaf!" . . . No malefactor had come to light, and everyone—even the unlikeliest people, even the widow Diligdisch, who was drop-sical and never left her house—was misgiving of where the suspicion might fall.

Newspaper accounts, although confused in some respects, did accurately report that Orvis had placed two bouquets on the Milfus front step.

Somebody up before daybreak had been witness to it.

And now that poor hostler began to shake. What if it was concluded that he, the father of two beauties, was ready to kill a man, a white one, for having showed them attentions? Lookalike bouquets at the front door could only have made reference to his lookalike daughters. When he learned that that hungry-eyed Mr. Orvis Truley had put the floral tributes there, Milfus had probably just lost all self-control and gone off to drown the wanton, the rounder. Milfus shook. Maybe people really would think that.

Orvis sat calm and mute at his brother's house—picking imaginary lint from his clothing, laughing from time to time, displaying brown teeth in bloodshot gums. But you had only to try reasoning with him, you had only to say, "Who did it?" and Orvis would put an admonishing finger to his lips.

In fair weather he ventured forth, voluble to himself, yammering steadily under his bad breath but cautioning to silence whoever approached. So far from being any longer a no-account figure of town fun, Orvis had through lunacy come into his own. Here came chaos, here came old night. People hewed to their best behavior, because they were afraid of him.

It was his little niece Velma, nobody's fool at age nine, who figured out first and by herself that Uncle Orvis had been his own malefactor. Through a knothole she'd watched everything on the evening, about suppertime, those nice young men had fetched her bleeding stupefied uncle into the lamplight. While her parents were busy applying poultices to the wounds and wondering aloud what kind of terrible world they were living in that such a thing could be done, Velma alone saw the quavering blue of Uncle Orvis's unshaved cheeks, saw him say with his lips though without any voice, "I'm sorry, everybody."

Murph smoked hard, waiting for Truley's answer. About the boathouse. It had an ingle where you could cook. It had a well out back with a working windlass. It had a plank bed (admittedly very uncomfortable—Truley had taken several nasty splinters from lying there). A man could live at the boathouse. Just supposably, he could.

"*Give* him the boathouse?" cried Truley. "When what we ought to be doing is calling the law? Let me at that telephone!" She crossed into the hallway with big strides. She unhooked the receiver. Fiercely she cranked, then waited for the familiar voice. "Hello, Central, put me through to—"

But right behind came Murph to snatch away the earpiece and hang it back up. "Suddenly we're an armed camp, we're scared of strangers? You listen to me, girlie," she said. " A stranger's got rights too, kind that aren't written down anywhere. And they're *all* he's got. I say the proper thing is to march ourselves out onto that porch and give directions to Offatts and say, 'Mister, you make yourself snug as a hen in pease-straw.' I say that's the proper thing."

"But for how long, Etta?"

"For the duration." Meaning: this was an old man, a conspicuously old man.

Miss Truley gave, after hemming and hawing, her customary one-shouldered shrug—of assent. You might as well argue with a switch engine as Etta Murph once her mind was settled. Back out front they came now. Felix and the stranger had seated themselves in the front yard under a spreading box elder, beautiful in this season with its yellow keys shagging the limbs. Shadows played checkerwise on the faces of the boy and old man. And what was that held between them in the stranger's open palm? It might have been a miniature person, a homunculus. But in the stranger's open palm was no homunculus. Here was instead a finger puppet—of heartstopping verisimilitude, dressed in minikin finery and placing now an arm at his waist, bowing deep to greet the ladies. His lips were bloody red over random teeth, his tongue slewed out to one side. The mouth of a debauchee. He had a tallow complexion and scooped cheeks. But the eyes, two little furnace doors flung open, bade defiance. The ladies passed each other looks. "Is that thing alive?" whispered Truley. The finger puppet beckoned them down the front steps and across the lawn, spreading bedizened hands to indicate that Murph and Truley should come and have a seat, come and join them.

Bob, who had watched all this from under the house, scrambled forth to complete the circle.

Then, very calmly, the puppet took off his face—

took it right off, as if it were his hat, and revealed the plaster blank, the nothing underneath. He briefly rockabyed the tallow-colored visage in his arms, then with sudden unconcern handed it to Murph. From the black velvet folds of his robe he now produced a new face and tried it on.

Truley shook her spellbound head. "Felix, honey, that's you. Isn't it, Etta, isn't it just Felix all over?"

It was Felix, to the life. The puppet busily removed the miniscule rings one by one from his fingers, letting them drop into the grass, not caring where they fell.

Felix had thought his gooseflesh could get no higher. But then the finger puppet proceeded to remove his second face, his face of Felix, too, and handed it to Truley. So there again to behold—did you dare—was the featureless blank head, flayed to nullity. It twitched a moment this way and that, like a body when the soul flees, and was still. Schmulowicz withdrew his hand from inside the puppet, put the body without a soul back inside the lining of his overcoat. And thus, without warning, the spectacle was over . . .

Traveler, Halt!

Confoundest thing I ever saw," Truley turns to Murph that evening and says. It is late, close on ten. They have put out the light. Time for talking now, Truley propped on one elbow, Murph flat on her back.

"Explain it to me, Etta."

But what to say? On a certain afternoon of July, at the tawniest hour, in Galvez Island, the earth—the tilting spinning earth—was unearthly. There is no accounting for this adequacy, this splendor that overtakes you. You lack neither flour nor oil while the famine lasts. On a certain afternoon, at a certain hour, the earth is earth no longer, but a fragment of eternity. And you, greenhorn jest of time, are a fragment of eternity too.

Murph says: "Let's get up early tomorrow and go right out to Offatts. Let's bring him some good things to eat. Oranges. I will bet you a dollar he's never even tasted an orange."

In sleep and dreams the ladies lie spoonwise, then back to back. On their bureau, for hard evidence that they have not spent the afternoon, also, in dreams, two little masks, of age and youth. The cast-off meretricious gems remain in the grass for Bob to nose awhile, then lose interest in. He will bark and bark, skeptical, at a just-risen harvest moon—immense, dim, three-quarters, a crumbled loaf of gold at the foot of Winnie Street.

CHAPTER TEN

Bayou Conventicle

SCHMULOWICZ MOVED SHADOWLIKE about the boathouse. From his unstrung throat came now and then a ratchety forsaken sound. Outside his door, in a pot hung between andirons, a thin broth was whistling. Residence at Offatts had lengthened out to two weeks now. The ladies arrived each second or third morning with provisions. Afternoons, beneath the pelting suns of early August, Felix would turn up, in a proprietary mood. He regarded the stranger as his and the ladies' private source of wonder, an arcanum all of their own. He would come creeping, concealed behind cattails at the bayou edge, to observe the old man at his routines—drinking down the scalding soup, abluting himself in the brackish water, making now and then a high-pitched sound that was both laughter and tears. Sometimes Felix would discover the stranger moving his bowels or passing a urine brown as spittoon water. Other times he'd observe him dance and wheel about, the moose-colored duster fanning out from behind, the wintry set of his face waxing young again.

On just such an afternoon, crouched in the bulrush, Felix knew suddenly that he was not alone. Nervous ripple at the surface. Undulant coil emerging, saddles of black and brown, muscular, lithe, half under water, half up a stalk. Bullet head thrown back, viper mouth wide now to reveal the gorge, dreadful white, where a forked tongue played. Cottonmouth.

There wasn't time enough to remember not to scream. As Felix did the moccasin lashed out, deadly of aim. Cottonmouths will strike, if they can, on the face or neck or chest, the reason they are so to be feared. There is little remedy for such bites. The venom makes its way too quickly home.

Drinking liquor until delirious is recommended. Most die just the same, however.

There came to him a purity of fear. He'd been warned all his life about vipers. Through salients of sunlight, brightening and dimming now to his heartbeat, through the starspray of sudden pain, Felix saw Schmulowicz the stranger advance on him in great strides, snatch up the fiend with a hazel wand and fling him back to the marshwaters whence he came. This with the dispassion of a farmer pitching hay. He gathered the boy into his arms and walked back to the boathouse. Inside he lay Felix down on the plank bed, unbuttoned the print shirt, then proceeded to examine the victim's wound—deep, clean, nearly bloodless. And underneath, the knot of poison. Felix watched the stranger spit onto his forefinger and rub saliva into the snakebite.

"Mister, I'm scared."

The stranger seemed not to hear.

"Suck out the poison, mister. You're supposed to suck out the poison."

The stranger went on rubbing spittle into the viper marks.

"Help me," Felix said to him and then, *"HELP ME!"* to anybody at all who could hear. Would his miraculous stranger let him down?

He would not. Schmulowicz padded over to the grip, rummaged briefly, then returned with a little jar. He unscrewed the lid. It was a salve, Felix saw, the color of which he could not make out. Neither red, yellow, blue, nor any combination thereof. This salve gleaming jewel-like in its jar was of the color, nameless and unknown, which the Creator had withheld from creation. Schmulowicz rubbed a generous dollop of it into the boy's breast. And a calm (not the wracking shudders Felix had heard tell of) spread through him, ministering to him. With the last of consciousness he watched Schmulowicz watch him, youth recrudescing in the old man's runneled face.

Along about sunset, when Felix waked up, there again before him was the withered head, bent now in some new concentration. Without bothering to remove the shirt, Schmulowicz had been mending a double rent over the boy's breastbone. He would straighten up now and then, the better to admire his work. Indeed it was admirable—stitches so fine you could not discern them against the print of the fabric.

"Am I alive, mister?"

Schmulowicz took up the alphabet board. "A-l-i-v-e."

"I feel peculiar."

"B-a-d?"

"Not bad, no. Come to think of it, not bad at all."

"Y-e-s—n-o-w—y-o-u—h-a-v-e—a—s-n-a-k-e-b-i-t—l-i-f-e." He doted awhile. "I-t—i-s—b-e-t-t-e-r—s-o."

Schmulowicz jerked his head in the direction of the towpath, from which a sound of laughing contending voices came. There was light, too, a dancing circle of it cast by a swung lantern. Here were Murph and Truley to pay an unaccustomed evening call. They'd come all the way on foot: veiled, gloved, redolent of citronella.

In the deepening shadows of the boathouse, with just enough light left to see letters of the alphabet by, the stranger hastily adjured: "D-o—n-o-t—t-e-l-l—t-h-e—l-a-d-i-e-s." Still lying down, Felix gave a rapid nod of his head as they entered, Miss Truley leading the way, lifting her veil, crying out: "Pity the poor mosquito who applies to *us* for his dinner!"

"Supper," corrected Murph, bringing up the rear, carrying the lantern in one hand and a hamper in the other.

Truley pulled herself up short. "Child, what are you doing here at this hour?" Felix put on a demure look. Truley took the lantern from Murph, held it up to the boy's face, examined him closely, feeling his forehead for temperature. "Peekid thing, you are."

"Yes ma'am," he concurred, hands interlaced across the crown of his head, a gesture both the ladies loved. "I must be coming down with *la grippe*."

"*La grippe*, young man, is not what we worry about in the high summer," said Murph.

Now a different light had begun to flicker in the boathouse, augmented by each candle the stranger lit. He was stationing them all about—on the floor, the shelves, the windowsills.

Miss Truley gazed up at the waver and sway of shadows overhead. "Oh, my days . . ."

Bayou Conventicle

"Put out the lantern, Velma," Miss Murph said.

It was even lovelier.

From two sawhorses and a half dozen planks the stranger had contrived a stage, illumined now in the shifting light. Chairs and stools and a pair of upturned scuttles he'd arranged semicircularly to accommodate an audience. A faded dirty cretonne, thrown out by somebody and rescued by Schmulowicz, he'd draped from a corbel and crossbeam. Thus his theatre.

Now he smote his hands together.

"I believe the play is about to begin," said Miss Murph to Felix and Miss Truley.

On the planks smoke rose from a tiny cauldron. A couple of bowls—the halves of a robin's egg, really—lay side by side at the foot of a peach tree, two span high, which was coming into flower. Here was a world of smallness made clear by what it excluded. Simpler than the big world, yes; the big world excludes nothing and this makes the big world hard to see. But here in smallness dwelled the promise of a truth.

There came a scratching noise from under the platform. The proboscis of a horseshoe crab poked up through the planks. He lumbered on stage doing a side-to-side step. Ah, he wasn't a crab. He was a puppet wearing the carapace of a crab. Now he shed his shell and was a lovely white-faced lady. The proboscis, unwound, became a head of hair which he—no, she—proceeded to comb out with delicate fingers.

Looking to right and left, she put the peach tree under one arm, climbed into the carapace and sailed away. But here Schmulowicz snapped his fingers, summoning her on stage again. He pointed sternly to where the tree had stood. Red in the face, she put it back.

Schmulowicz now produced a little torch, put it into the lovely lady's hand and, pointing to the footlight candles, bade her light them, which she did. She held the tiny flame back up to him; he blew it out. Then she put the brand, still smoking, under her arm, climbed into the carapace and sailed away. But Schmulowicz snapped his fingers, summoning her back. He put a finger under her dress; she pushed it away. He glowered at her until she complied—hoisting her skirts, squatting, shuddering. At length, she laid an egg into Schmulowicz's waiting palm; and, in great weariness, went back to her carapace, lay down and slept.

There came a harried headless man on stage—his arms turbulent—rushing this way and that in search of what he lacked. After some groping about he found the egg in Schmulowicz's hand, fitted it onto his spindle neck and began to bang at it with his fists. Fragments of eggshell fell away, and now a miniature of the head of Schmulowicz himself was discovered. Big Schmulowicz offered little Schmulowicz a hand mirror into which little Schmulowicz gazed, not without admiration, picking the last bits of eggshell from off his head. He looked and looked, growing vain. Then big Schmulowicz snatched away the looking glass and broke it.

Now little Schmulowicz rushed over to the lovely lady, asleep in her shell. Wake up, wake up. He needed for her to admire him, love him, see that he was beautiful. Wake up. She would not. She only turned over. Wake up. Big Schmulowicz intervened, removing little Schmulowicz's head, putting it in his pocket. And that was that.

The lovely lady turned over, stretched, yawned,

arose; but she was no longer lovely. She was a bird of prey, indigo-plumed and with a hooked beak. Her head jerked nervously, as if a quarry were near. Oh, terrible. Then she flew up, perched herself on the crossbeam above the stage—freed (it seemed) of the puppeteer's mastery. But the life was draining out of her from the moment she took wing. She had flown, and where she had flown she stayed: humped on the crossbeam, quite, quite still, because dead now.

Schmulowicz produced a little flagon of milk, shook it vigorously. A handsome young man appeared, stage left, arms outstretched, begging for drink. Schmulowicz denied him. The handsome young man came to Schmulowicz and tugged at his sleeve. Schmulowicz relented, offered the flagon. The young man drank half, handed it back. Schmulowicz drank the rest. Now the young man began to smile and unbuttoned his shirt to reveal an eyelid in the middle of his chest. The eyelid opened to reveal a rose garden. There were red blossoms and yellow and white and blue and, at the center of each, an eyelid opening to reveal a rose garden with red blossoms and yellow and white and blue.

Whether or not the play was to have ended thus is uncertain, for there came a two-handed pounding to dispel the illusion. "Open up in there! Open up, I say!" Finished or not, the play was over. And whose fists were these on the boathouse door? Who was this crasher? Deputy Sheriff Bill Purvis, Jr.

Miss Truley knew the smiling face of trouble when she saw it. "Why, hello there, Bill." She'd been all through school with this slouch; had the measure of him long since. "We've got a pickup meal here in the hamper—baked chicken parts, fried okra, and a cold potato dish. You're in time to join us, Bill."

"Quite the little party," he said.

Schmulowicz was meanwhile attempting to edge away into darkness, his Bedouin stare never leaving the deputy.

"And here's fine company for you gals—a little boy and an old man. Humph! You'll die wondering, both of you."

Truley's cordial tactic was clearly not going to

work. "State your business," Murph said evenly and took off her hat to reveal the high forehead, built for thinking.

"Maybe Deputy Purvis would like to see the show," Felix chirped. Miss Murph and Miss Truley passed the boy torpid looks, so he said no more.

"Show? Somebody around here putting on a show?"

"State your business, sir," said Murph.

"My business is with that jewbird you gals is keeping out here. Bureau of Immigration got the lowdown on him. They say he don't belong here in Galveston. Say he belongs in Fort Worth."

At the mention of the dusty one-eyed burg of Fort Worth, Miss Truley's and Miss Murph's least favorite on earth, they let out a gasp and a moan respectively.

"Say he's got to head on up there p. d. q."

"Why don't you go to Fort Worth yourself?" Murph asked, signalling an end to all civility.

The deputy sheriff's leathern eyelids snapped shut. "I ain't about to mince words with a hinny," he said, indicating Truley, "and a mule," indicating Murph. "Or is it the other way round? If I was not a gentleman and here on strictly legal business," he added, while the hand in his pants pocket, on business of its own, re-arranged his groin, "I'd tell you both where to go. It wouldn't be Forth Worth neither."

"Am I wide of the mark, sir," Felix put in, "to surmise that it would be Hades? Hell is of course a Judeo-Christian conception. Hades, also called Dis and Avernus, is the classical equivalent. Or not really equivalent, inasmuch as—"

"Who pulled your string, young feller?" asked the deputy. And blinked again, iguanalike.

Now he brought out a sheaf of official-looking papers and commenced to read aloud: "Wherefore it is stipulated by Mr. Jacob Schiff of New York City, benefactor of these immigrations of Russian Jewry to the port of Galveston, Texas, that each immigrant of adult age shall receive, prior to embarkation, an assignment of gainful employ in a city or town other than Galveston—"

"Why *other* than Galveston, I would like to know," said Miss Murph.

"Evidently, they got Jews out the back door in New York and Baltimore and Philadelphia. They got all the Jews they need up there. Know why? Cause these folks get to town, find their own kind, and then they stay put. Help each other out, don't you know? Talk their own language, follow their own customs. And what have you got before long? A ghetto, I believe they call it. And a ghetto we in Galveston don't need. No, thank you, ma'am."

Murph shifted her weight, put a hand on one hip. "Who is this Mr. Jacob Schiff—to be making people's decisions for them?"

"Richest Jew on earth."

Here Felix listened up. The deputy sheriff's last utterance didn't sit right with him, who had always assumed his grandfather Mehmel to be the richest Jew (if not, indeed, person altogether) on earth; this only stood to reason, seeing as Sweet Brook Brewery was earth's most lucrative enterprise. Wasn't it?

A noise of violent coughing halted his reflection.

Truley rushed to a darkened corner where Schmulowicz had dropped down. "Having one of his fits!"

Murph hastened to re-kindle the lamp. She held it up to reveal Schmulowicz in a heap on the floor, his head lolling forward. Truley said, "I'll bring him over there." And she picked the old man up, just picked him up no different than if he were an armful of laundry. Indeed he did not weigh more than that. "Like carrying a ghost," she murmured. But Truley was not afraid of ghosts.

Or deputy sheriffs for that matter. "Bill Purvis, clear the table so I can lay this sick man down." And he did as Truley told him.

Schmulowicz's seizure began to subside. He lay still, eyes glittering and black . . .

Now he closed them.

"Deceased! Deceased!" cried Bill expectantly, looking round the room.

But no. One hand was fluttering randomly at the stranger's side. This shook Murph to see, this hand—this elemental puppet, the one inside of all the others—jerking about like a trammeled thing. The stranger opened his eyes.

Now his hand steadied itself, began to point towards the foot of the plank bed.

"He wants his alphabet board," Felix said, crossing the room to fetch it.

A sudden dose of pain showed forth in the old

man's face. The Bedouin lustre of his gaze closed up into wrinkles, the bloodshot gums came into view. He made the sound that was both laughter and tears and, taking up his board, asked:

"W-h-a-t—a-m—I—t-o—d-o—w-i-t-h—t-h-i-s —b-o-d-y—o-f—m-i-n-e?"

Murph pulled a horse blanket from under the plank bed, shook it out, covered the stranger up to his chin. Truley opened the hamper and took out a vacuum bottle of pear cider, a cup of which she poured out. "Raise his head, Etta." The stranger drank. A trickle ran down his chin and onto the blanket.

Felix reached for the handkerchief in his back pocket and patted the stranger dry.

"Man's in a bad way," said Purvis, Jr. "Needs a doctor. I could have sworn he was—"

Murph glanced up, as if it had slipped her mind he was present, then curtly returned her eyes to the stranger. "We've seen him through several of these sinking spells ourselves. Can't say as a doctor would do better by him than we have."

"Man needs a damn *doctor!*"

But here the stranger swivelled his head in the

dcputy sheriff's direction. His lower lip protruded, then relaxed into a grin. Same as always when death was mentioned, as Miss Murph had noted in philosophical colloquy with him. Issues of life, death, and eternity were Murph's stock-in-trade. The stranger freely obliged her, hearing her views; would now and then spell out one of his own. Together they broached the question of whether there was a beginning to all things, and if there was a beginning to all things then what was there before that; and the question of whether souls are immortal, and if they are immortal then do they transmigrate from incarnation to incarnation or are they embodied only once; and other such noble questions.

"Y-o-u—k-n-o-w—w-h-a-t—I—a-m?—H-u-n-g-r-y," said Schmulowicz and Miss Murph's stomach let out a rumble of agreement. Miss Truley reached for the hamper.

Thus it was that they came to break bread with the enemy. "I'm here on strictly official business," the deputy reiterated. "Don't suppose a snack ever hurt nobody, though." He ate for four, leaving one single thigh of chicken for Murph, Truley, Felix, and Schmulowicz to dine on as best they could. Bill loudly praised the potatoes, prepared in a German fashion, but could not forbear adding that the okra was not up to what *his* little woman made. He drank down the last of the cider.

Couldn't you *just*—!" Truley snarled when the law stepped out to have a pee. She lifted Schmulowicz from his chair, carried him over to the plank bed, lay him down. "Get yourself some rest, old-timer."

Bill came back inside, took a seat, cleaned his fingernails with a knife. Returning to the table, her back to him, Miss Truley produced a deck of cards, these being what she enjoyed when the evening meal was done. "Slap pack, anyone?" As always, Felix accommodated her. As always, she would win. Miss Murph, who didn't care for games of cards, rinsed off dishes in a pail of water. Schmulowicz slept . . .

While under their noses the evening changed, grew turbid, surcharged. A great southerly awning of cloud, the look of heavy weather in it, uttered now a downward fork of lightning.

Felix left off playing cards to count out softly to

himself: "One one thousand, two one thousand, three one thousand, four one thousand, five one thousand, six one—" Came the leisurely thunder peal.

"Looks like a foul turn of weather, Bill Purvis," said Truley. "I mean no Presbyterian rainfall. I mean a *Baptist* downpour. If I was you, I'd get on back to town."

"Not without who I came for," he answered, pledged to obstinance. "It's my job to do."

"Do you have a warrant?" asked Murph.

"Didn't think I'd need one. Thought he'd come peaceful like."

"You'll not be taking him without a warrant."

"My instructions was plain enough. Bring this Smoolywits back to town."

"But you'll not be taking him without a warrant." Murph hazarded a couple of steps towards Bill. Involuntarily, he stepped back.

"How about if he dies? How about *that?*"

Murph stepped forward again and Purvis back, losing ground, stumbling at the threshold. Now she'd got him out the door, which was her purpose. They stared each other down in darkness, the wind blowing rank and laden around them. A greenish sheet lightning showed Murph and the deputy to each other. One one thousand, two one thousand, three. Came the clap of thunder, close on.

"You want the *responsibility?*" Purvis bellowed. "It'll be yours!"

The wind was salt on their faces.

"William Purvis, Jr.," Murph said quietly. "Shut your ignorant mouth."

CHAPTER ELEVEN

Looking for Snowies

AT THE OTHER END OF OFFATTS the storm had broken now in earnest. Yet Peter Munger and Albert Roache were dry, having spread a tarpaulin, the kind used for covering hayricks, over the leaky roof of their treehouse. They lit the spirit lamp, climbed into sleeping rolls, listened to the pounding on the canvas.

"I'm telling you he wouldn't," Roache said.

"I'm telling you he would, and he *did*, the old snoop," Munger replied. At issue was the identity of an intruder who had climbed the rope ladder to their fastness, rifled through their belongings, even made free a little, it seemed, with their whiskey. Munger's opinion was that the trespasser was none other than Leo Mehmel, their sponsor. "Hell of a note," he told Roache, and turned his back, and went to sleep.

The following afternoon, while delivering a bicycle for Mr. Fewtrell, Munger glanced up to second-storey windows of the Tremont House. There stocking his bird feeder was Leo, who waved excitedly when he saw Munger. Munger swept his cap from his head and bowed low.

"Come up for tea, won't you?" called Leo.

"You bet I will," Munger called back. "You bet I will, Mr. Mehmel, *sir!*" Leaving the bicycle in the care of the concierge, Munger mounted to Leo's apartments.

In customary *deshabillé* the latter answered his door. Munger flashed the give-nothing smile and strode past, brushing hard against Leo.

"I ain't up here for your tea and cookies," was what he turned and said. "I'm up here to warn you."

"Beg pardon?"

"Warn you to keep your mitts off our things."

"I haven't any idea—"

"*Haven't any idea,*" echoed Munger, harshly mimicking. "Lookahere, me and Al is aeronautical *geniuses*, you see? It's your good luck, Mehmel, to be helping us along. Chance of a lifetime, I call it. Grab yourself a place in history. Not as big as ours, of course. But what we do not stand for is some sneak, no matter how openhanded with his money, gumshoeing up the rope ladder when we ain't at home."

Leo grimaced. "You're mistaken, Peter."

"Prove it."

Leo considered the matter, pushed forth his pigeon chest. "I'll stake a lookout," he declared. "I'll discover who these trespassers are. Have they stolen anything?"

Munger narrowed his eyes. "You sure *you* don't know?" But the tone mixed dudgeon with uncertainty. He was backing off now from his hothead allegation.

"Quite, Peter."

"Stole several swigs of good bourbon, whoever it was," Munger said, aggrieved, preferring now to stare at his shoes.

"Not an irreplaceable loss, Pete . . . See here, I've got some birding to do out that way. Suppose I keep watch of your place at the same time?"

Next daybreak he rose, ate a bran muffin, washed it down with camomile; strapped on field glasses; confided the bird ledger, an apple, an orange, and a flask of water to his rucksack; and set off for the aerie dwelling of Roache and Munger.

The young men had devised, not far from their treehouse, a makeshift hangar where they kept the partially built flying machine; they'd made excellent progress on it, working late by light of firebrands, their arms and faces smeared with insectifuge. Despite significant overruns of the original estimate, Leo had continued to subvent them. Materials were vastly more expensive than Roache had supposed. Every few days he would come to Leo, hat in hand, and ask for a further advance of capital.

To what extent this was straitening their benefactor neither could have guessed. Leo's creditors about town, always promptly compensated in the past, wondered why now his obligations went unsatisfied, why he responded to their duns with partial payment or none at all, content merely to write letters making unspecific promises about the balance due. There were bills for the fashionable clothing—poplin suits, batiste shirts, Haitian cotton scarves; bills for the fresh-cut flowers, delivered every fourth day to his rooms; bills for the everlasting millet and sunflower seed stocked into the feeders; bills for the opulent meals taken in solitude at various eating establishments about town where he would consume supper very slowly, preoccupied by an ornithological tome open to one side of his plate.

But it was too late to back out now. Work on the glider had progressed to a point where Roache and Munger were emboldened to announce an exhibition for the Labor Day weekend. SEE A MAN FLY! read the public notice they pasted up on the Strand. Townsfolk gathered round to express fascination and—naturally enough—skepticism.

Leo had uppermost in his mind that morning to visit a nest of bitterns, concealed among canebrakes, that had contained six olive-colored eggs when he found it the week before. As he approached this morning the father bird let loose his customary protest, a splitting *oong-KA-chunk! oong-KA-chunk!* Not wanting to get too close, for the father would swoop menacingly if he did, Leo contented himself with a glimpse through the brakes. What he could make out, using binoculars, was three newborn chicks, blind and glabrous; and their mother bustling among them, holding her craw open for the babies to eat from.

Now he heard a noise that made him turn the field glasses skywards. Veering above him was a sudden throng of boat-tailed grackles crying *jeeb-jeeb*, then settling, all of them at once, into the crown of a cottonwood. Handsome sight.

Oh, there was a sufficiency of marvels that morning: a Louisiana heron, a seaside sparrow, a mottled duck or two, a dashing flight of gull-billed terns. But none of these was what Leo Mehmel had come to see. No, he was in search of that heartbreaking bird, the snowy egret, pursued nearly to extinction for a fine plumage. For snowies show in the mating season a long lacy feather upon the dorsal side, suitable for trimming a lady's hat with. Alas, you rarely saw a specimen anymore—even here in Galveston, crisscrossed by flight lines, beloved stopping-off place of birds. Other sorts of egret were plentiful, but no snowy had been sighted since the year of the Great Storm.

Leo felt for those living anywhere else. Here was the beulah land of bird watchers, second to none on earth. Restlessly in every season the species came. He stopped to note in his ledger those just seen. Only then did he permit himself to think on the human connection which had brought him hither: he'd promised to stand watch of the treehouse. Bending his steps now that way, he came to a hedgerow wound with trumpet creeper where he was fortunate to observe a ruby-throated hummingbird, stationary but for the whir of wings, drinking nectar from a blossom, flying up, backwards, down, hovering insectlike, imbibing again. Leo took out his ledger, noted down the specimen.

When he got within view of the treehouse, he saw that the rope ladder was down. Strange to say, Leo only now felt tempted to commit the trespass of which he'd been falsely accused. Merely scaling with his eyes those rungs held by knotted ropes, a savor of guilt coursed through him.

In the minute or so required to wade through a field of bunch grass and get to the tree, his heart pounding in his throat, Leo determined that, yes, he would make the climb. It was the boys' treehouse, perhaps, but not their tree, he reasoned. That live oak and all the land for acres around belonged to one Mrs. Thigpen, an abstractly goodhearted widow of means who left the ground fallow and let it be known that common folk were free to come and go on her property as they wished. The only forbidden thing was hunting. Every hundred yards her land was posted: HUNTING FORBIDDEN BY ORDER OF CAMPASPE THIGPEN, FREEHOLDER. There was a picture of a rifle with an X over it for those unable to read words. Officers of the law had instructions to bring all who were apprehended there to the old widow herself for a tongue lashing prior to their arraignment—unless the malefactor happened to be Negro, in which case Mrs. Thigpen's hearthside corrections could serve no purpose (the dark race being morally unimprovable) and were accordingly dispensed with.

Looking for Snowies

As Mrs. Thigpen had posted her acreage, so Munger and Roache posted the treehouse. A bold-faced placard ran as follows: KEEP OUT, YOU ROTTERS! BY ORDER OF PETER MUNGER AND ALBERT ROACHE, AERONAUTS. But Leo rationalized, midway up the rope ladder, that the live oak was Mrs. Thigpen's after all and that therefore he could climb it. He knew what a graceless figure he cut, not at all like Roache or Munger sprinting up the rungs. But the going was easier today without his beneficiaries watching, holding back their mirth. He pulled himself through the hatch, sparing his shins this time. All was shipshape—sleeping rolls tied up, utensils stowed. They lived with the rigor of seafaring men, these boys in a tree.

Leo looked around, said, "I love Munger and Roache." Again, full-voiced, with feeling: "I love Munger and Roache." And he passed his hand over his mouth, and he sat down on the floor.

It was not long before this pleasure of trespass yielded again to guilt. Leo climbed down to the surly earth below. He was getting hungry so he took the orange from his rucksack, peeled and ate it, slaked his thirst with water from the flask.

On he trudged in a circuit round Offatts. The bayou lay as if asleep, gathering summer light. The sun by that hour was high and hot. The air was close. Leo broke a sweat all over. He passed various farmsteads and came to a towpath. He saw the little boathouse abutting a stand of bulrush. He walked right up to the window and, cupping his hands to his face, peered in. (Munger was right, he *was* a snoop.) A gnarled little man lifted his eyes from what he was doing. Leo recoiled; this was his first view of Schmulowicz and it sufficed. He hastened away, the mirror of the bayou glaring after him as he went. And fish crows—that bad lot, that no-account species and nuisance, according to Leo— flew up from the bulrush to jibe at his going.

Caw! Caw!

He headed back to the treehouse but stopped to watch some type of acrimony between a red-headed woodpecker and a starling. Resuming his way, he halted again for the fair sight of twenty or more scissortailed flycatchers—coral-colored underplumage flashing as, with harsh cries and snaps of tail feathers and high-flown arcs above the half-acre of scrub growth which was their proclaimed ground, they fulfilled the elate and careless nature of scissortails.

Kee-kee-kee-kee!

It was to marvel.

Leo continued his circuit, coming again by the other approach in view of the treehouse; and saw that, lo, the rope ladder was up. He sought higher ground, then took a look through his field glasses. Oh, now he had that trespasser dead to rights! But how to proceed? Should he rush over to Fewtrell's and inform the boys? No, that would take too long. Should he make what is called a citizen's arrest? Well, frankly, Leo had not yet got a look at what type of person this intruder was. He might be dangerous—muscular, armed with a weapon, etcetera.

Leo peered awhile through his field glasses; he could see nothing. Suddenly, in the southern window of the treehouse, a flash of arms, naked backs, two heads of hair. Then nothing more for a minute or two. Then, the face of his nephew Felix looking unmistakably back at him.

What was the apple of the eye doing up there?

Leo and his nephew had always been resistant to each other, opposed magnets, and now he remembered with renewed humiliation the time five years ago when an unpleasant thing had happened. "Give your Uncle Leo a kiss goodnight," Lucy had said. Felix did so but afterwards pulled a face and wiped his mouth on his pajama sleeve. Lucy followed him into the hall to hiss a reprimand the content of which Leo, sitting embarrassed in the parlor, had been unable to catch, though he well enough heard what the boy shouted back:

"He makes me *sick*, that's why!"

To be thus loathed by a dead brother's issue is not nice. After several minutes, Lucy came back into the parlor. "I declare that boy's coming down with something."

"Fresh mouth, I'd call it." Leo was attempting to feign amusement. But Lucy saw that he was hurt.

"Forehead just burning up, teeth chattering too! He'd never have acted that way otherwise. I put him right to bed. Don't please give another thought to what he said, that was just a fever talking. Because the boy's devoted to you, Leo, *devoted!* One morning he came down to breakfast and said to me, 'You know, Mother, I think I'd like to be just like Uncle Leo when I grow up.'"

Which was absolutely true, he'd said it, though Lucy didn't add that, quick as he did, the boy tossed his head to one side and howled with laughter. Or that despite herself she'd laughed too. Once you have been singled out as the family mortification, jests and jeers acquire a life of their own, wonderfully self-sustaining . . . And unsuspected, often as not, by you yourself. Relations are kind; the derision goes on out of earshot of you. Felix didn't like his uncle. Leo was scared of his nephew. These two facts abided. And so the latter did not go down to the treehouse to yell "Clear off!" No, he turned and made his way home. And his heart went around like a dory in a squall. And when a brace of snowies flew past, trig in their summer plumes, Leo did not see.

CHAPTER TWELVE

Round the Bend, Up the Straight

LUCY DID NOT WONDER how two such siblings as Aharon and Leo had sprung from one source. This did not seem among life's mysteries—no more, indeed, than the polar variance of herself from sister Molly. There had come from New Orleans the previous week a fine long letter to report spells of measles and whooping cough passing harmless through sister's brood; mewlings and pukings of the very youngest; fits of moody noncooperation lately overtaking the eldest. It did seem to Lucy that some basic impulsion, granted aplenty to a "twin" sister, had been withheld from her. The talent for maternity, the rudimentary urge of it, she herself was unpossessed of, whereas with Molly there was the hearkening in blood and bone, an untutored drive to mother.

Several years running now, the latter's plans for a visit to Galveston had fallen through owing to this or that unforeseen circumstance. With eleven to tend, it was scarcely to be wondered at. Molly would each time send a note of apology accompanied by the latest photogravure of herself and hers before a painted studio backdrop of Jackson Square Park and the Basilica and the Father of Waters flowing by. "I'll be down to you next year, make no mistake. Would you just *look* at me, what a old biddy I am. I tell you what, it's *funny!* Send along a picture of you and Felix, quick as ever you can. I bet you haven't changed one bit. You're still pretty, aren't you, spite of it all. What I want is to see how that poor only child turned out. Rest your Jewish husband, honey, but I do hope the boy favors you and not him. Because we've got some Jewish right here in the neighborhood, and I don't like the way they look. I'm sorry, but that's my opinion."

Lucy hadn't got round to having that photograph made. Lucy, in truth, got round to less and less. This fine midsummer morning, a Saturday, it was not until ten thirty that she turned her hand to anything. A long circular rumination preoccupied her. Seated at her dressing table, pale as an Easter lily, eyes on herself in the mirror, she said the words "a blindfold life," for that was what she lived now.

It was that she had no church to go to. That was her problem. The padres at Saint Mary's Cathedral told her that her worship was not welcome there, that her baptism had been made unbaptism by conversion to the Hebrew faith. A travelled man and proud of it, Monsignor Fogarty made a small mouth and described to Lucy two figures adorning the western façade of Notre Dame in Paris, France: the one *Ecclesia*, Holy Mother Church, Bride of Christ, with orb and diadem and sceptre; the other, *Synagoga*, with broken staff, fallen circlet, blindfold eyes.

"It's she, my child—she, and not the Lovely

Lady—whom *you've* chosen. I am sorry for you. I grieve."

"Father, hear my confession."

"Impossible, Mrs. Mehmel, under the circumstances. You are a Jewess." His shift from "my child" to "Mrs. Mehmel" particularly wounded. Would Lucy, in her need, be denied even this bare consolation? It helped to be called "my child."

Monsignor required a cane (sometimes two canes) to support himself. This on account of an ulcerated foot, which cannot have been helped by the heft of the man. Quoting her the letter of the canon law, he had difficulty in controlling his spittle, Lucy observed. Be canon law as may be, it did seem that he took a spacious pleasure in refusing her. "Let the peace of mind be ne'er so great," he declared, "it is a fallacious and blindfold life if that peace come not from our Savior Jesus Christ, who shed His blood at Calvary and ransomed us from sin . . ." And so on, dilating further.

Lucy interrupted to say, "I've no peace, father, of any kind," and got again his high-nosed snub. "I'm the prodigal come back. Why don't you know me?"

"Know you? I know you for an excommunicate.

I've a sorrowful instrument to that effect from the
Bishop of New Orleans. Why, it's now more than
fifteen years ago I received it, but a priest remem-
bers; it is not often, you understand, that such a
measure is inflicted. You've said before that you
would like to see the documentation? Mrs. Mehmel, it includes a letter of disownment from the
hand of your late father, whose Christian heart you
broke. You've no peace? I shouldn't wonder."

Canon law provides for *latae sententiae*—that is,
official—excommunication in cases where there
is apostasy from the one true faith in order to
espouse another. It is as simple as that. Particulars
may include getting yourself married by a minister
or rabbi, letting your children go unbaptised,
depriving them of Roman Catholic instruction,
etcetera. Lucy understood that a sheep like herself
could now return to the fold only if she brought her
lambkin with her. Monsignor had explained, time
and again, all of this—at first patiently, later less so:
that the Church must regard her as contumacious
until such time as she underwent the sacrament of
penance; but that before Holy Mother Church
could proffer the reconciliation, her child must be

baptised. Monsignor explained that there could be no other means of absolution for her.

Familiar enough, all of it heard before, heavy tenets which had lain a long time in the cellarage of Lucy's soul, making an evil ache there. But she could not, except in dishonor of a dead husband and his living parents, see the issue of her marriage baptised. Each time she reiterated this the monsignor tucked his chin into his throat, smiled very gravely, said there was not more to say.

"I have the honor, Mrs. Mehmel, to bid you— good after*noon!*"

But today she was armed. "Monsignor, not so fast." She loosened the drawstring of her bag; she pulled the weapon out. A Bible. She leafed through to Luke. She read to Fogarty about the prodigal's father, about what he said: *Bring forth the best robe. And bring hither the fatted calf. And let us eat, and be merry.* And so forth.

There ensued a silence, very grim. Monsignor's foot was hurting. Lucy heard the rasp of air as he inhaled now, and watched his twisting brows.

"Anyone may quote the Bible, Mrs. Mehmel, anyone at all; and this is why we of the true priest-

hood do not, like ministers, encourage the dissem-
ination of Holy Writ for general reading purposes.
Far seemlier is it that we Roman Catholic priests
read aloud *to* the faithful. Scripture is a sacerdotal
trust, Mrs. Mehmel, and we do not hold with just
anybody carrying it about *in her handbag!*"

Monsignor Fogarty came from County Roscom-
mon—in the Irish midlands—and he had the Ros-
commoner's way of gulping back the words a bit as
he said them. Odd to listen to, along with his ster-
torous breathing. Lucy began to cry.

Fogarty raised two fingers of blessing a moment,
as if involuntarily, then caught himself. It seemed
he was confusedly of a mind to fold her in his
arms. She could see him for the first time as a man
and see what kind he was beneath the holy orders:
one of those who cannot bear to watch a woman
weep.

"Take this blindfold off," she said. The Presby-
terians, the Methodists, the Baptists would have
told her to take it off herself. Convenient. But
theirs was no true faith, no more than the blindfold
denomination with which she had tarried. At day's
end Lucy and the sententious prelate were of one

mind: there was the Church of Rome, and the rest was error.

Catholicism had meant little enough to her when she left it. Empty forms. But now, in shipwreck, the ancient hunger and thirst came back: *To eat of this body, which is given for you; to drink of this cup, the new testament in His blood, which is shed for you . . .*

The longing for it had made her strange—to feed on that mystery, God in the mouth. Lucy Mehmel caused murmurs when, unwelcome, she would appear at Sunday Mass, genuflect and cross herself, enter a back pew and kneel to pray. Communicants wondered if she would be so bold as to approach the altar for the Blessed Sacrament. And what would poor Fogarty do if she made such an attempt? Deny her, to be sure. But what if she were a spectacle? What if she upset the Body and Blood of their Lord onto the stone floor?

Or what if she outraged the Mass by shouting something aloud at the warders of the Host?

"Pharisees!"

None of this happened, of course. Bewitched to her huddled heart, Lucy only knelt and prayed.

She'd started off so well with people hereabouts—
the Jews, the Protestants too, if not the Catholics,
who were poor anyhow, negligible in society,
inhabiting the shabby hinder end of town. But in
her widowhood, it seemed, the quality one by one
had dropped Lucy Mehmel. She would see by the
social page that So-and-So had given a lovely
party—her invitation to which would somehow not
have arrived. Old friends when they happened
onto the relic of Aharon Mehmel would be no less
friendly than of old, but their conversation did
tend to center on how busy they had been and
would remain foreseeably. And wasn't it a shame
one found so little time for paying calls nowadays?
Taking rapid leave of her, they would swear to pass
by as soon as their busy schedules allowed.

What, meantime, did they say behind her back?
That the household at 2422 Broadway—or what
remained of it—was a wild and peculiar household.
That the elderly Negro woman who'd come from
New Orleans with Lucy was in effect mistress now,
domestic matters devolving on her because Lucy
could not cope with them. That her and Aharon's
only child had been allowed to revert to nature and

lived like a raccoon cub or young possum: desultory, investigative, out at strange hours, and so forth.

Neither rumor was true, strictly speaking; nor again was either quite false. Each suggested the general disorder to which life was tending, not the specific state of affairs already achieved. It must be said that Neevah *had* taken over considerable of the household decisions. It must be said that Felix in these changeless weeks of summer *did* run increasingly to the wild. When Neevah tried to remonstrate with the boy, he would stare blankly back at her.

"I knows trash in whichever color," she said more than once to Lucy, "and trash is what the child done took up with." A reference to Wick, who'd not fooled Neevah for long with his smarmy ways. She had overheard quite another Wick, the second or third time he came to the house, saying things to Felix which couldn't on any interpretation have been nice, things Neevah didn't care to repeat. Just very dirty. But there was something worse, there was humiliation going on, Neevah perceived. She'd heard Wick enter Felix's room and say, "Hi, slave," a very odd greeting. She'd heard him call Felix "nigger" and "nobody." She'd heard him call Felix "doormat."

Once, she'd heard him call Felix "queer bait"—a phrase that took some figuring out, though was certainly not beyond her, for nothing was.

She'd heard Wick ask Felix, "Where the hell's your self-respect?" She'd heard "butthole," she'd heard "pussy," she'd heard all she could take.

"What you going to do about it?" Neevah asked Lucy. "Have yourself another dose?" Laudanum was what she meant. Lucy took a patent brand of the drug—Phillansbee's Guaranteed Pick-Me-Up —to medicate her sick headaches. *"For Ladies!"* said the label of the square-shouldered brown glass bottle. *"A Bracer! A Refresher! A Reviver!"* Nothing else seemed to work. She had found herself more and more reliant on the tonic which, though harsh, could be made palatable by admixture of two parts wine. To say frankly, her "headaches" had become a manner of speaking. What she medicated was a general and inclusive pain. Here is how, on a daily basis, it proceeded. She would note a building loneliness as the afternoon wore on. She would know a primitive need to hide, yet not be able to. Or there would come a clogging of the air, a mustering coil that choked her off. She would flee to an armoir, close herself in. She would know this choking by other names: sin and guilt and shame. She would emerge to pour herself a dram of Phillansbee's Guaranteed and wine; another and another, until sleep.

Memory played her false. Waking to moonlight, she would not know if it was early or late. And what had become of the previous day? Dazzled to dimness, her mind's eye stared. Particulars fell away, leaving only a general sense of life as with the speed of a millrace rushing from her. She cast about, at last remembering something: she had a son. Was this the harbinger of worse, to have it slip your mind you had a child? Now Lucy saw her way clear, saw round the bend and up the straight. "I won't go there, I won't go there."

But how not to go? Phillansbee's Guaranteed. And wine. She mixed herself another; she drank it down. The first of day was paling up. A pheasant shrieked. From her many fine dresses Lucy selected a plum-colored affair, crepe de chine shot

with blue. A very odd rig it was for a Sunday morning, what with the deep neck and the bodice in a
pattern of cabochons. She let her hair hang down
anyhow and over it, with the effect of old-fashioned
ways, placed a shawl of black Belgian lace. She put
on cloisonné bracelets, three of them. She put on a
double strand of pearls with a tourmaline clasp. It
occurred to her to add a brooch, a garnet sunburst.
But hadn't she neglected earrings? She removed
the shawl and added earrings, a pair of amethysts
in fluted gold.

And now, as if a little girl again, Lucy decided to
put on all the rest of her jewelry. Rings three deep,
brooches pinned here and there, bracelets up both
arms, a great collar of necklaces beleaguering her.

Too much? She took an appraising look in the
mirror and thought not. Trailing the black lace
absently in one hand, she went downstairs and out
to Broadway. She turned to see sunrise flooding the
eastern face of her house, and heard the pheasant
shriek again, and watched him take his flight.
Palms along the boulevard shook their spiky heads,
for a turbid breeze was up this morning. From one
of them a huge frond fell suddenly in dry rattling

bayonets to the ground, nowhere near to Lucy, though near enough to provoke the thought of how such a death would do. Bang! on the head; or maybe pierced through, impaled, it was not impossible.

What would monsignor say then? He'd be sorry. Tears brimming in his pale and ruddy eyes, he would confess that there is no end to the mystery of grace, that he'd been the one with the blindfold on. The widow Mehmel's pathetic shawl, dragged through the dust? Miraculous, deserving of a reliquary to house it.

Lucy had wanted to be a saint for some time now. This ambition overtook her in the course of a single day, September sixth, nineteen hundred. Until the Great Storm she'd not looked back, had wasted no care on saints and such—not excluding the little Syracusan martyr whose namesake she was. Feast day of Saint Lucy each December? Meant nothing. Who cared?

But the widow years were another story. She recollected more and more what a sister of the Ursulines had once told her: if you are afraid of the Father, pray to the Son; if you are afraid of the Son, pray to the Mother; if you are afraid of the Mother, pray to Saint Lucy. Such are the recourses of polytheism. Lucy Mehmel had lately made the most of them, recalling with solace the four categories of sainthood: those known to the Church, the duly beatified and canonized; those not yet canonized but who will be; those never to be officially canonized, whose sanctity is disclosed to family and friends but not to the Church; last of all, those known for now and all time to no mortal, only to God. Imagine it—that skinny waitress who served beer to the loutish crowd of the Sugar Bush alehouse—madman Orvis Truley all the day picking imaginary lint from his garments—Filipe, stripped to the waist, planting bearded iris—McClung, putting fruit jerky out in the sun—the wet-eyed mulatta cutting silhouettes on the Strand—those pleasant young men who fixed bicycles at Fewtrell's—vile old eloquent Fogarty, even he. Mightn't any one of them be—well, what? A savior, after the manner of Christ. Wasn't this the difference between the world of now and the world of before He came: that in the aftermath there could be lives imitative of His own, suffused, sainted; that in this aftermath the ongoing miracle of sanctity, with two legs and two arms and a beating heart, could cross your path and make you new, take away sin as had the Lamb of God when He said at Genessaret, "Follow me," and Peter and James and John, transfigured boys, dropped their mended nets and went?

Imitatio Christi. We ordinary ones can't do it. Enter the saint, therefore. He might be the unlikeliest person—say, for an extreme hypothesis, that Mrs. Gernsbacher, the rabbi's wife, mail-ordered carping hypochondriacal thing. But who for a certainty was to deny her the gift of Christlikeness? Who was to conclude that Rivka Gernsbacher wasn't a Christian saint? She?!—a Jewess and etcetera the bunch at Saint Mary's would put forth in objection. So what? If the mystery of grace was as vast as they claimed, mightn't the rabbi's unpromising wife be a saint, just mightn't she? "And if Rivka Gernsbacher is a Christian saint, then so can I be."

Thus Lucy rounded off her train of thought—which was in truth dissolution, crack-up in the nerves.

At this early hour few people were about. In diamond whorls the mist was passing off from the dawn. A milkman turned on the box of his wagon to stare at Lucy, who astonished even his limited sense of how a high-class lady ought to dress at daybreak. Had she worn that crepe de chine—a souvenir from married times—to an evening party it would have only looked out of mode. But taking into account the surfeit of jewelry, and taking into account the early hour, it looked worse than out of mode, as even a milkman could see.

She'd waked up from a bad dream in the twilight of that morning, waked to blankness, could remember nothing, knew only that what she'd dreamed had made her coldly sweat . . . Now, in the way of dreams, what was lost came back unbidden, and she is alone in darkness, riding some sort of raft, face down and clinging for life, pitched by breakers she can feel the weight, height, and terror of but not see. Against the winds she raises her head to behold for an instant just what the ocean is made of. Not water. As if by the sputter and flare of a struck match she glimpses instead—human beings, wave upon wave of the slack-mouthed, open-eyed dead. And for all of them she must somehow bear the blame. Her fault, her fault. Until she saves them all, this great storm cannot end.

Lucy walked north on Twenty-first Street as far as the Cathedral. She entered, late again for early Mass.

"*Hoc est enim corpur meum.*" Staved up by acolytes, Monsignor Fogarty was pronouncing the consecration. "*Hic est enim calix sanguinis mei, novi et aeterni testamenti: mysterium fidei.*" Fogarty spoke the Latin words in rapid stately monotone. Glancing up to see Lucy take her seat in the last pew, he paused a moment, sighed deeply. The least an excommunicate could do, he felt, was arrive on time to Mass. "*Qui pro vobis et pro multzs effundetur in remissionem peccatorum.*"

Here Lucy tried-but failed—to catch a hiccough; it came right out, the way hiccoughs do when you're pitifully drunk, and resounded.

Viola Claffey, wife of a local salesman in hardware, kneeling across the aisle from Lucy, bent to her husband and said, in a wrathful stage whisper, "I had *heard* she takes liquor!"

Imagine being decried, censured, moralized upon by Viola Claffey, a woman like that, a woman who snored even when not asleep. Very well: Lucy would now do what she came to do, would show them all. She took from her bag a real weapon this time, a pair of pinking shears, and in one two three four strokes, blades flashing as she wielded them, cut off her raffia hair. It fell onto the green velvet of the pew, onto the floor. Gasps came from close by to where she knelt. A sniggering child in the row ahead got duly smacked on the neck by its mother. Monsignor halted the final doxology. Viola Claffey let out an original sound, something between a snort and a squawk.

Later that morning, following this shameful episode at Saint Mary's, policemen brought the inebriate home. "Child, what have you done?" Neevah cried, taking a look at the poor head, knowing this at once for a desecration Lucy had committed on herself. The crepe de chine? Dusty and wrinkled. Had she been in some type of struggle? Thus it seemed. What these officers of the law told Neevah—who stood round-shouldered in the foyer not daring to respond by so much as a word—was that her mistress would have to stay at home from now on, that behavior of her kind was not going to be tolerated in public.

Bill Purvis, Jr. was there, the best of the lot, the only one with sense enough to remove his hat.

The law took their leave now.

Neevah watched them from the front door as they disappeared down the drive and out to Broadway, then turned her face, harsh with pain, to Lucy. "Get you a wash, get you some of that mutton soup from the larder, you be *fine,* child." She slipped an arm round Lucy's waist as she walked her up the stairs. "You just tired out, thas all," she said, her voice clotting in her throat. "*Tired out!*" Lucy made no response.

Neevah undressed her in the upstairs bath. Pacific, yielding rag doll—Lucy's was the body of someone not there. Neevah took a wet cloth to her neck; the dirt came away in streaks. She bent her over the bathtub, poured out water from a pitcher onto the hacked-off hair. Filth from Lucy's head turned the bathwater brown. "Oh, I can't get you clean, child. Need a tub bath. Need a soak."

How had she got so *dirty*? Here is how: sextons were obliged that morning, in the aftermath of her demonstration, to take Lucy out by the strong arm. She'd clutched at the pew, had had to be pried away, yelling the while, words jumbled without a meaning. Outside she'd pulled free, flung herself down in the dust of Church Street. Her pearls when she grabbed at them came unstrung and rolled away higgledy-piggledy, some breaking under the sextons' shoes.

After Neevah had bathed her mistress and washed her hair, and put her into nightclothes and carried her to bed, and built her up with pillows, and covered the shagged-off head with a night bonnet, and drew down the window shades, she called out for Felix, sleeping up the forenoon.

Why, it was nearly ten. All of him Neevah could see above the bedsheet when she entered his room was the feather edge of a recent haircut. "Wake up, baby. They's trouble in this house."

Felix yawned, stretched, turned over. She hadn't a doubt this was the laziest child ever to draw a breath of air. In no state of mind to put up with him this morning, she yanked Felix upright. He

shrugged a moment, then remembered his naked-
ness. He grabbed for the sheet.

"You think I care? Just pull them clothes on,
them that's on the floor. I need you to set with your
momma. You hear? Cause your momma can't be by
herself."

Felix, tetchily: "Can't be by—?"

Neevah gave a doleful shake of her head. "Don't
be backsassing me this morning, baby. I ain't got the
time."

Felix sullenly followed to the bedroom of his
mother, still buttoning his pants. Neevah's big hand
pushed him through the door and shut it behind
him. A late morning sun filtered in through drawn
shades. He stood with his back to the wall, at the
farthest from Lucy, who lay quiet now.

But she under whose watch he had moved was
not there. The mother comfort, the assurance of
her, relinquished bit by bit, the early familiar to
which he'd clung, the spell of consolation—gone.
Here was what remained, the integument.

Felix knew now what he knew. She'd not get well.
He remembered coming through the front door
that winter to see dusty smithereens of the old

scale model—kept up in the attic, and with which he'd sometimes played when younger—littering the checkered floor of the entry. She'd flung it from the landing. McClung had seen her, though Lucy, defending herself, hollered, "Innocent! Innocent!" Told Neevah to stack up some Bibles and she'd swear to it. "As many as you think necessary— borrow from up and down the block!"

Lose a father and you may imagine that the blow has fallen, that you are safe. Or you may think twice; and know that, early or late, we are thus picked and picked clean. Felix bounded for the door, getting as far as the hall only to meet up again with Neevah's crisscrossed hand. She took him by the collar, thrust him back in. "You do like I tells you."

In the attitude of watch and ward, eyes narrowed with pleasure, Hildy crouched beside Lucy, kneading at the bedclothes, snagging the bedspread in her claws. Felix compelled himself to sit down on the slipper chair opposite, buried his chin in his hand, stared.

"Badness of kitty," he said. Through the years of

unreflective usage this strange phrase had got to be routine. Badness of kitty.

Felix reached out, touched the sleeve of his mother's nightgown. Here was the new hour, marked upon the dial. Here was what happens. The years do their work. Such knowledge—as yet too big—yet was in him: discovery, relentless as arithmetic, not to be denied. He said, "Mother," then "Lucy," though wept no tears. Interesting to call your mother "Lucy" instead of "Mother." It granted the momentary release from being who you were. For who you were was familial: Father, Mother, those headwaters. But who you *really* were was—unfamilial.

An extempore courage stirred in him, the long-headed train of thought now heaping itself into a question: How do I, starting from these others, become myself? He bent to his mother, loosened the pink ribbon, took the sleeping cap off of her head. He looked around the room for fear but could not find it. The shorn head ought to have sent him fleeing, but did not.

Years from then, miles from there, an old man

believing in nothing but what memory granted, he would recall two days most: the day his father disappeared into the weather; and the day, seven years afterwards, that his mother cut off her hair. Events which, taken together, should have made a plot: the king disappears into a cloud, the stricken queen cuts off her hair. Here was entailment. One garnered the sense of it. Things like this (or similar to this) did happen.

And could be borne, once you'd wrested the story from them. But now, put a gap of seven years between the king's going and the queen's grief. Randomness. You had no tale at all.

Felix looked about the room for fear but could not find it. Was this what all our rage for telling meant? To surmount randomness with a story. To guess from outcomes the long way back. To learn thereby hidden causes. To be scared—well and good—but not scared to death. To go on the errand into randomness and return with the tale to tell. First "this," then "that." And "that" only as the necessary consequence of "this": only by entailment did stories work. Figure Aeneas fetched up in Carthage, too scared to say to Dido what befell. Figure him, Aeneas without his plot, blubbering, desultory, struck to incoherence, denied his high fate, which is to be elsewhere and otherwise and to do the boldest thing. Aeneas did not blubber. Gazing round Dido's great hall for fear, he found instead his story . . .

Then be like him; tell the human tale.

King disappears into a cloud. Seven years pass. Queen cuts off her hair. Ah, randomness. No story at all.

Try again.

King disappears into a cloud. Wish it though she may, Queen cannot grieve. So something worse than grief carries out the slow revenge. Now Felix felt a nethermost wind urge him on from there. He kissed his mother, asleep in the opal half-light of her room, and went out.

Hildy mewed and followed.

CHAPTER THIRTEEN

Slow Note Due

NEEVAH WOULD ORDINARILY have gone to the back door of the elder Mehmels' house at Sealy and Sixteenth. But this noon she walked up the front steps, knocked repeatedly, said through the screen when Liselotte answered:

"Miss Lucy done took sick in her mind."

That was all. Liselotte said something back which Neevah could not understand, foreign words, and clapped a hand to her mouth. She motioned Neevah indoors and into the parlor where old Gerson sat in a wicker Bath chair, his mouth worn to one side, a pair of smoked glasses hiding his eyes. "Stay with him," she instructed and went to the alcove where the telephone was, cranked the mechanism, asked to be put through to Gernsbacher.

Rabbi and Liselotte had the habit of speaking to each other in English, as was customary among the little colony of German Jews there. Today however she recurred to the old language.

"Rabbi, Rabbi, bitte kommen Sie sofort wenn es ihnen nur irgendwie möglich ist." She'd not identified herself, but he knew at once the voice, ragged now with what it implored.

This being Sunday the telephone call found rabbi out of harness—undressed though it was noon, wandering the house in but his night drawers and sock feet, Frau Gernsbacher in a wrapper ghosting wordlessly past him. Into this marriage of rabbi and rebbitsin the great silence had lately settled. Done now with hectoring, Rivka poured out only her disregard—onto rabbi and onto sundry of his belongings: the telephone, for example, a device she'd not wanted in their home to begin with. But rabbi had insisted so as to let congregants reach him more quickly in what he called their "spiritual emergencies." Home alone, Rivka would cross her arms, turn her back, and allow the detested inconvenience to ring and ring.

"*Was ist denn los, Frau Mehmel?*" Gernsbacher asked into the mouthpiece.

"*Ich kann am Telephon darüber nicht sprechen, Rabbi. Können wir uns bei meinem Sohn treffen?*" He wondered for a minute whom she meant. One son was dead, after all. The other? Unmarried, putting up at a hotel. About him the less said the better.

Now Liselotte clarified, in a voice cleaving apart: "*Es betrifft meine Schwiegertochter.*"

Ah, then, the daughter-in-law, the young widow. "*Selbstverständlich, Frau Mehmel, komme ich sogleich.*" He went to his bedroom, shook out the trousers of his gray serge suit, stepped into them; put on a glazed shirt and celluloid collar; laced up his brogans. Without benefit of a mirror he knotted his tie, reflecting on the unsuccessful call he'd paid to Lucy Mehmel a month ago.

Would another rabbi have pled better? he asked himself. One, perhaps, keeping better custody of his eyes. Over and over, speaking to the widow, Gernsbacher had looked away; but his gaze had reverted to the alabaster neck, delicate hands and cinched waist of a woman who, though buffeted by life and no longer young, was still formidably lovely. And here he was, ancient enough almost to be her father's father. Only one dignified thing to do with an emotion such as this—take it to the grave with you. Thus Gernsbacher's self-reproach.

Under the impress of his last conversation with Lucy he had sat down and opened himself to the full and terrible glamor of the alien creed. Yes, he had read their so-called New Testament.

His opinion?

Highly overrated . . . Though it must be said that when rabbi put his head to the pillow lately, he would hear choirs of *goyisher* angels caroling their good news. And see kneeling before him the lovely widow Mehmel, a slow smile lighting her face, who poured out oil from an earthen jar and began to wash his feet.

Shameful, he'd told himself each time he remembered the dream. Shameful and *lightminded.* This latter epithet sprang often to rabbi's lips. Was it not a proof of rigor that from time to time, in the grip of unclean thoughts, he could turn it on himself! Was not self-disgust the forecourt to

righteousness? These the ruminations of a man
knotting his necktie, who waged the war on light-
mindedness—*Leichtfertigkeit*, the fundamental trait
of gentiles, as he believed—wherever it sprang up,
even in himself.

But a doubt rose against him: could such self-
reproach be only another ruse of pride? It was here
that, like a phonograph needle, Gernsbacher's
reflection stuck: of pride, of pride, of pride. Did
not any conviction of one's own righteousness
imply it? Was there no way out of the vicious circle
of oneself? The prophets said yes, of course—and
called the way *teshuvah* or atonement. You returned
from waywardness to the commandments of God,
you followed what He dictated, you refrained from
what He forbade. You knew you were righteous
because you obeyed. Plain enough. But if repentance was thus plain and prescribed, was it really
repentance? When Nathan Gernsbacher made
teshuvah he found himself feeling only too good, as
if unimprovable, as if one touch of the Creator had
translated him, a provincial insignificant rabbi lost
in this vast New World, to Jacob's bosom where the
righteous go home. Then he would own a suspi-

cion that it was Samael, prince of darkness, not the Lord God Almighty, who'd done the leading on—and decoyed him, poor fool, into complacency.

There were those (a majority, indeed) who said that religion was solace. Peace to them, but it was not. It was, rather, the succession of intractable doubts. For might even the abjectest obedience be yet another ambush of egotism, for these were endless? Now Gernsbacher passed to still bleaker suspicion. Might there be no Creator no Revealer no Redeemer at all, no Lord our God who is One, commanding us to be righteous? Suppose a world thus divested, where demons throng but He is not, and ask what can our righteousness be? Vaunted wish, figmented hope. Round and round Gernsbacher went, sickening on the wheel of doubt, looking about him as he whirled, seeing people and places as they must finally be: Galveston a necropolis ruined to rubble, frequented by the cottonmouth, the screech owl, the hyena. He knew himself—none better—for what he was, a pettifogging rabbi who'd lost the faith of his calling.

Gernsbacher put on a snap-brim hat with a broadcloth band, affronted himself briefly in the

mirror of the entrance hall, then took ignominy
out onto the street. A costermonger peddled wares
of the season door-to-door. From the other direction came a hosing cart down the middle of the
road, sprinkling water to lay the summer dust.
Gernsbacher forged through the heat of that
noonday, raising his hat to neighbors as he passed
them, and came now to the widow Mehmel's house
on Broadway. Liselotte stepped out onto the front
gallery and without a greeting began to tell him in
rapid German of what had happened. He noted at
once her decided Berlin accent with, underneath, a
trace of Posen to it. As a youth he had certainly
uttered just such a German himself, the bright
sleave of Jewishness threaded through. This was
simply and involuntarily how one spoke having
come from Tarnopol to Posen and from Posen to
Berlin, as her people had. Or from Kalish to Breslau, as had he. It took a generation and a half of vigilant self-consciousness to train the Yiddish residue
out of Jewish German speech. Even then, with slav-
isms and hebraisms expunged, word order recti-
fied, consonants roundly enunciated—even then,
at times of stress or hurry, the old undersong came

Slow Note Due

back, as the stain which seems gone from a carpet will reappear on humid days. The generation of Liselotte's and Gernsbacher's parents had immigrated in prodigious numbers to the cities from the villages, shedding *Yiddishkeit*, finding themselves in the fullness of time more German than not, keeping only oddments of the old ways. While deep in mind's ear—there to listen for—echoed dimly the outdated grandparental wisdoms. "A shroud is not made with pockets," or: "Send a lazy man for the angel of death," or: "Sleep fast, we need the pillows." *Shtetl* adages, pensioned-off now. "A Jew's joy is not without fear" and so forth.

Liselotte showed rabbi up the curving stair to Lucy's room, darkened against the day.

"For pity's sake, give her some air, some light," Gernsbacher said.

Neevah, keeping vigil at the bedside, looked up. Like live coals her stare dimmed, brightened, seemed to breathe. It was she who'd lowered the sash and drawn the drapes. What did he know about remedies! Lucy needed still air and darkness. Also silence, so why was he talking? She put a finger firmly to her lips. She glared.

Who else was in attendance there? McClung and Filipe, joined in prayers for the swift recovery of their mistress. McClung covered her eyes with one hand and fingered a rosary with the other. Filipe bowed his head, crooked hard brown hands in supplication.

"But where is the boy?" whispered Gernsbacher to Liselotte. A reprehending downward turn of the mouth was all of her answer. Rabbi looked to Neevah, saw the fading flaring eyes. She rose laboriously, tall enough to face him. "I declare that child want no part of us," she said. "I done tolt him to stay right here by his momma. And when I come back with Miz Mehmel, what do you think? Baby's gone, which is the usual. Turn your back a minute, baby's gone from here."

What is there in the way of comfort for such a household? Rabbi condoled as best he could with Liselotte, promising to return that evening. She clutched him by the coat sleeve as he made for the door. The old wrathful eloquence had mostly deserted her; she made do now with the plain words of one reduced from indignation to fear.

Slow Note Due

"Don't go yet. Sit with me." She gestured to the bedsitting room across the hall. "I'm by myself too much now." She shut the door behind them. "And with too few opportunities for talking." They seated themselves and were silent. Liselotte had the collected look of one who has thought something through to its finish.

"Have you ever wanted to go back?" she asked him at length. "Myself, I have never, not even on a visit. What for? Every cobble and brick is in memory . . .

"I was eight when we came from Posen to Berlin. Papa's work brought us. He'd been offered a post as head tailor of the Grünfeld Department Store. Rabbi, did I ever tell you about him?" Liselotte was dressed very simply today, as always—a white lace gorget on a brown piqué shirtdress. Also, a long strand of amber beads, worn in a knot, which she absently fingered as she spoke. "My father died standing up, hemorrhage of the brain—can you imagine?—while measuring somebody for a suit of clothes. He put a hand to his brow, said, 'Excuse me' and died." She tucked a stray tress of hair back into her chignon, patted her forehead and upper lip with a handkerchief. "He'd asked in his will to be buried at Posen, in the Jewish cemetery there, ancient shady place—I dream about it. Each *Jahrzeit* we'd return, Mama and I, to lay a pebble on the headstone of the grave. Something comes back from one of those visits. I was curious about a particular monument in the park, very important-looking, larger than the others, surmounted by an arch. But it had gone to ruin. The base was cracked, the keystone missing, the whole thing overgrown with moss. With difficulty, I made out a surname. I asked Mama what she knew about them. 'That's a family that doesn't exist anymore,' she told me. What did she mean? I wanted to know. Had they literally died out? Or had they simply lost their place in the world, returned to insignificance? My questions irritated Mama. Possibly she thought it bad luck to speak of such people. Still, without knowing more, I knew enough, enough of what can happen. That name on the broken arch, that was a people for whom life had become too hard."

She stood up, calmly prophetic. "It is happening now to us."

Getting to his feet also, rabbi fumbled for what to

say. "Fortunately, you possess means to obtain the finest doctors." This was the lamentable best he could manage.

"Means?" Liselotte asked. *"Means?"* Evidently she did have a wag left to her tongue. "Through misfortune, through improvidence, through neglect, *we have none!"*

What, the fabulous Mehmels? How could that be? Beyond what it took to establish the roof over his and the rebbitsin's head, Gernsbacher had remained a man uninterested in money. It was one of the many shortcomings his Rivka tasked him with. Unattracted to sums larger than required to live on, he assumed that those who did possess fortunes knew how to tend them, how to make their great sums greater. In this New World the rich got richer—didn't they?—as if it were no whet of good luck but the deep-down nature of things conspiring to back them up.

Yet suddenly the Mehmels were—well, what? "Bankrupt," Liselotte said. A manner of speaking, wasn't this? Liselotte shook her head. A temporary deficit in accounts? Liselotte gave it to him plain: what had been a very going enterprise now looked receivership in the teeth. A slow note at the bank, on which monthly interest had been paid, was due presently for the principal.

"This, this *showplace* you see might have remained the working capital of a profitable business. Heaven forbid!" said Liselotte. "And what have we got to show?" She jerked her head in the direction of Lucy's room: "*That*—that is what comes of profligacy!" Rabbi clutched his hat in both hands. Unrabbinical though the feeling was, he longed only to flee. "Look at me, a woman with no help. One son, dead. The other, giving away money with both hands. Lucy, Leo, Felix, my husband, myself—we take and take from a shrinking source. The fact is, rabbi, we are unable to re-finance our note. Inroads into capital have been too great, the banks say. 'Unworthy' is what they call us now. Oh, I do what I can. I hire men to manage; always the same story—thieves, tricksters who turn profit to loss on the ledger! They tell me a vat must be replaced. I give them the money. No vat is replaced. And what happens meanwhile to the product?"

It goes to hell. Sweet Brook Lager, once the finest

beer in Texas, had degenerated into something undrinkable. "Since we are speaking of this, and speaking so frankly, Frau Mehmel, I must tell you," said Gernsbacher, shifting from one foot to the other, hands in his pockets, "that I myself, once a loyal drinker of Sweet Brook, have regretfully gone over to the competition."

"It is so, then—our product is inferior?"

The truth wanted out. Rabbi bowed his head, spoke low. "Not what it was, Frau Mehmel, I regret to say."

Now Liselotte wondered why she'd summoned him. To hear this? She remembered glorious sermons from the man, silk off a spool. A rabbi was meant to have such words in readiness, wasn't he? And to want to speak them, giving solace? Gernsbacher wanted only the door.

He reiterated his promise to return that evening. He sketched a bow and took his leave.

Yes, Felix had set off at a score, a strange double-minded feeling hastening him away. What had he told himself? That he would go to the stranger for some of that medicine in a jar, ineffable of color, mysterious of effect, with which to comfort his sick mother. But here was the greater mystery: on the way to Offatts he forgot her. Call this the ruthlessness of youth. Call this whatever you like, but his bicycle and he, by some connivance between them, traveled in the wrong direction, due north to Wick's house, instead of west to the bayou.

It must be said that Wick Frawley, that bane of Felix's existence, had improved upon better acquaintance. For the price of three dollars, raised with difficulty over almost a month, the school-days tormentor had metamorphosed into the boon companion of summer. Now a member of Wick's club, Felix was pledged to all duties, entitled to all privileges. They did lots of things together, gadding off on westward pursuits. Town itself held no more mysteries. But the other end of the island, this was a different story. There they found a tree-house in the shape of an aeroplane which, though posted against trespassers, tempted them as a shelter from the midday heat. They would take off all of their clothes once they got up and flop down for a rest. Books about aviation were there to peruse. Also a deck of Mexican playing cards, the reverses of which showed men and women in fifty-two love positions. Wick and Felix found some sour mash whiskey to try to swallow down.

Not least, they found their own naked selves, electric to each other's touch. Really, such pleasures were what each day they hurried up the rope ladder for, though neither would have said so. Wick and Felix had sealed a tacit agreement not to speak of what their bodies did together. These undeclared things happened—fifteen minutes here, fifteen minutes there—in planetary pauses, intercalations off the clock.

So feature their dismay of an afternoon to find the floor hatch of the treehouse thrice padlocked against them and a strongly worded sign hung from the rope ladder: FIXED YOUR HASH, NIGGER!

"Somebody thinks we're a nigger," Wick explained.

Other purlieus beckoned. That fallow field with a disused barn at the edge, near to where a stand of sweet-gum grew. The boys had peered through chinks in the locked door, trying for a look at the phenomenon inside. Inferring the whole from the part glimpsed, Felix posited a great winged moth, cocooned in darkness, thinking hard, plotting its freedom. A shaft of sunlight from a cranny enabled them to make out what appeared to be steering levers. Felix turned very slowly to Wick. "Do you know what we have here? Do you *know what we have here!?*"

"Sort of like the treehouse, right?" Wick answered.

Felix shook his head in grim dismissal of the treehouse. "That *make believe* up there? That *caprice?*" Came the ten dollar words now, as always when Felix was excited. "Herein is no whimsical imposture, but a bona fide flying machine, *the article itself!*"

Felix grabbed at the padlock on the door of the hangar and shook it with sudden unreasonable strength. Astonished, impressed, Wick could only wonder at the quicksilver change. "Let me in there!" Felix cried.

Now Wick tapped him on the shoulder. "Two men is up yonder," he said nervously, pointing to the stand of sweet-gum. Ignorning him, Felix continued to yank at the padlock. "Come on," Wick urged. "Let's get out of here!" He gave a tug at Felix who turned to see his sometime persecutor in a state of fear.

Roache and Munger stood at the rise, a striated sky behind them. *"You get the hell away from there!"* Munger hollered, his voice dim in the head wind. Now he and Roache were running full tilt at the boys.

"Come on for your life!" Wick cried, scrambling for his bicycle, unsteady at the handlebars, dashing up sand and pebbles from under the wheels. Whereas Felix, disdaining all panic, actually stopped to remove a sandbur from his shoe before mounting for the getaway.

"Stay off, too!" Munger flung after the boys, unable to catch up to them.

Roache panted at the air. "They're just pups . . . Shouldn't cuss like that at them, specially not on the Lord's day."

"Oh my, oh my," said Munger, rounding on him. "Suddenly we got us a creeping Jesus." He stepped back in sham reverence. "Always good to have one of them on a job."

"I only meant you should curb your tongue a little," Roache said quietly, and fished in his pocket for the key to the hangar. It worried him no end, this way Munger had of going off at half-cock. How would he behave tomorrow, Labor Day, before hundreds who would crowd these fields to witness the much-advertised flying exhibition? Realistically, Roache hoped for no more than a five- or six-second glide of the biplane, and at modest altitude. Whereas Munger, bent on an unfading glory, had declared he would loop-the-loop for openers, then clear that stand of sweet-gum, coming to rest in Mrs. Thigpen's far field. The crowd, said Munger, deserved no less.

"You'll be doing no such of a thing," Roache had told him. "And you'll be promising me here and now, or else we don't go no further with this. A simple straightforward glide."

"Alright, alright," said Munger, turning from him with a smirk.

"Your word, Peter?"

"My word, Al." But then, vaguely, under his breath, "Except if I forget."

Now they hauled her out, airfoils showing brilliant white. She promptly took dominion there, lightsome, nimble, friendly somehow, a new thing under the sun. Today's task was to fly her as a kite, unmanned. They checked the craft for tightness and for balance. They tied on guy lines. They pulled her at a run across the field until a light air caught under the silk of the wingspans. Slick as a whistle she was up, lofted on a thermal, gathering the warm air under her wings. Below, Roache and Munger felt they might be hauled at any moment from the ground. She pulled like a whale at their lines. Mad with pleasure, Munger began to climb his and had to be admonished by Roache.

"You'll *unbalance* her, Pete!" The glider listed ominously. Roache gave a hard compensatory tug to his line and brought her back to trim.

From two fields away, where Felix beheld this great sight, he dismounted his bicycle and stood a while, swaying with the wonder of it. There surged in him a vastness as if—suddenly—everything of life were barging through. And he was grateful for this floodtide, though he did not know what it meant. Coming to himself now, he realized that he'd begun, at last, to cry.

And Wick? Wick had fled for all he was worth,

not looking back. When finally he did and saw that Felix wasn't behind him, he only reluctantly circled round. "What you standing there for?" he asked, then saw Felix's wet face, shiny as a buckeye when he turned. "You okay?"

Felix considered the question a moment. "Never better," he replied, and this was only the truth, for what the boy beheld had put a nameless calm in him. The glider slipped now behind a tree; Wick hadn't even seen it.

"Well, come on then, we got us things to do." Wick re-mounted his bicycle and pedalled in the direction of the wagon road. Serene now, as if indemnified—feeling indeed that he'd grown a set of wings from his shoulder blades—Felix followed. Where the road ran out they picked up the path to the boathouse and, arriving there, flung their bicycles onto the hummocky ground.

"Did you get what that was out of your eye?" Wick asked, a little hesitantly.

Felix only nodded.

In the doorway, over which a beggary of dog roses had lately bloomed, Schmulowicz stood to greet them. Just that morning Murph and Truley had been out to him with foodstuffs for the larder: fruits, a cheese, vegetables, a loaf of bread. "Velma, the Hebrew nation are fanatically strict in their dietary regulations," Murph had explained a couple of weeks earlier, and spelled out the strange particulars. These made Truley shake with laughter.

"What's so funny, may I ask?"

"Two days ago, when I came out by myself, I pulled in a big old catfish, and I cleaned it and fried it up for my lunch. You think he didn't want any? Ha! A *trencherman*, he was. Told me afterwards, on his little board, you know, he didn't think there was a thing on earth could taste any better." Armed with such evidence, Murph and Truley had not scrupled this morning to bring Schmulowicz a smoke-cured ham, delicious, which they placed in the larder.

There had remained a second matter for Nathan Gernsbacher to see to that day. He hurried to the stable at Mechanic and Seventh where, courtesy of certain congregants, a buckboard and roan mare were kept at his disposal. He instructed a stable hand to prepare the rig and to harness the mare who, when led forth still chewing a mouthful of oats and passing salvos of wind, looked shyly from under her forelock.

"Fine animal, sir," said the stable hand, fastening the traces in the hames. He stroked her busy jaw and kissed her on her muzzle. Now Gernsbacher handed the boy four pennies of drinking money, hoisted himself into the buckboard, lashed the mare lightly, and was off.

His errand was delicate, touching a certain scofflaw, or person alleged to be by the Sheriff's Office. Deputy Purvis, Jr. had telephoned in some upset to inform rabbi that Yankel Schmulowicz's papers were not in order. Reluctant to detain him owing to the man's great age and poor health, Purvis wondered if rabbi would be so kind as to settle the matter. "Looks like his choices is two. You agree with me, reverend? Death or else Fort Worth." Fort Worth was as good a name as any for the dung heap of life; here was a fellow with a way of putting things, Gernsbacher thought.

Where the road ran out about two miles from

Slow Note Due

Offatts he came to a sandy path with a ribbon of green up the middle. Followed, it led to the boathouse. A westering sun ran gold and verdigris in outlying fields. Thistledown passed sidewise through the streaming air. Rabbi hobbled his roan and strapped a feed bag onto her. By the wayside he noted a pair of bicycles flung down on hummocky terrain leading to the rose-covered door of the boathouse.

"How do you do?" he asked into the gloom, fanning himself with his snap-brim, adopting the clerical tone. Three livid faces looked up. No reply. "May I come in?"

Smileless as any beast, Schmulowicz rose and came to the door. Rabbi gave a start when he saw him, then drew himself up and summoned a formula or two in Yiddish to suit the occasion. "Let me introduce myself—Rabbi Nathan Gernsbacher, from Breslau, in the Prussian province of Silesia, but an inhabitant for thirty-four years of this fair town of Galveston. I am, you may say, the elder of our little Jewish life here." How he'd learned to loathe his first tongue, this Yiddish—so slack, so bastard-sounding. *Zhargón*, he called it, the term favored to mock and stigmatize *Ostjuden* speech. Rabbi deliberately imposed on his Yiddish an occasional change of word order or pronunciation, thus to present himself as one who, acquiring *mamaloshen* solely for the sake of his rabbinical duties, had come to it from good graceful German.

Alas, if he'd thought to deceive the stranger; Schmulowicz stripped rabbi to his rudiments with but a look.

Wick now stepped into the light, handed the stranger his alphabet board, exchanged nods with him. "What's a matter, mister?" he asked rabbi, passing setter eyes up and down him, making a comely frown, waiting for no answer before turning away.

"Y-o-u—w-o-u-l-d—p-r-e-f-e-r—G-e-r-m-a-n—I—t-h-i-n-k.—O-r—e-l-s-e—y-o-u—w-o-u-l-d—p-r-e-f-e-r—E-n-g-l-i-s-h," said Schmulowicz to Gernsbacher.

So it was just as Deputy Purvis had reported—the stranger talked by spelling out words.

"W-o-n-t—y-o-u—p-l-e-a-s-e—c-o-m-e—i-n?"

Slow Note Due

Wick had seated himself before the proscenium. The other boy Gernsbacher knew well enough once his eyes had adjusted—Felix Mehmel, truant in a family crisis.

"I was with your mother this noon, young man. Imagine my surprise to learn that you, the man of the house, were absent from her bedside. My purpose in coming here was not to find you, but it is fortunate that I have. Hurry home at once," Gernsbacher admonished him, "where you are required!"

Felix's gaze flickered cooly. He said nothing, not caring to make a right impression, not on this officious person, justly bitten by Hildy on the nose. At that moment Gernsbacher embodied for Felix the whole regrettable world of the grown-ups. Doubtless he was here today to make some grown-up mischief. Would the stranger let him?

Rabbi said to Schmulowicz, "I urgently must speak with you on an official matter, of the utmost importance—"

With that Schmulowicz smote his hands together.

"Show's fixing to start," Wick declared, setter eyes flashing. "You're going to *see* something, mister!"

"Wick, give him the best seat in the house," Felix said, all wiseacre magnanimity now.

Gernsbacher reiterated, a little weakly, to Schmulowicz: "Official matter—utmost importance—"

"Take a seat, sir," Felix said, and rabbi did as he was told.

In the time required to lower and raise an eyelid the puppet stage is a barrens of snow. Thus the spectacle begins. A young man wearing a cloak and laden with books, each about the size of a postage stamp, comes on stage. So bookish is he that his head is book-shaped. He sits down in the madding whirlwind, puts on his glasses, begins rifling through tome after tome. Schmulowicz taps him on the shoulder. Don't bother me, the scholar seems to say, pulling his cloak tighter about him, reading further, faster. Now Schmulowicz gives him a shake. From under his tongue the puppeteer produces for the snow-clad scholar another book, smaller than the others, emerald color, and offers it. Everything whitens now: books, cloak, hair. At the heart of the whirlwind the tiny book shines, wrapped in an emerald flame which burns but does not consume it. The young man opens the fiery text, pores a while, then lifts hectic eyes of green, for they have caught the blaze.

As if on command, the blizzard stops. Fire fades from the scholar's eyes, then from the tiny book itself. Schmulowicz applies a miniscule sponge to the young man's face, wiping away the proud bloom from his cheeks, the lustrous darkness from his hair. In a trice he is old. His book-shaped head wobbles on his shoulders . . .

Oh, this had been but the beginning. Schmulowicz's play told a long and ramified story. The little stage was vast that day, compassing decades, continents. When finally the spectacle ended Gernsbacher was aware of a throbbing in the pulses, a ringing in the ears, an uncanny hunger that gnawed him. All strength to move had deserted his limbs. With the rheumy eyes of a hunting dog who's seen hard use, and known privation, rabbi sat and stared.

Wick meanwhile had been whistling a little tune, of improvised composition. Today was his first exposure to theatre, and he'd enjoyed himself capitally.

In obedience to a silent behest from the stranger, he and Felix now set about preparing lunch. Schmulowicz approached Gernsbacher for a confidential word.

"I—n-e-e-d—o-n-l-y—o-n-e—m-o-r-e—d-a-y.— T-w-e-n-t-y—f-o-u-r—h-o-u-r-s—a-n-d—I— w-i-l-l—b-e—g-o-n-e.—S-h-i-e-l-d—m-e— u-n-t-i-l—t-h-e-n—I—u-r-g-e—y-o-u," he said and flashed a glimpse, there and gone, of the young face folded into the old.

"You and I . . . can we have . . . met before?" Gernsbacher choked on the words, fell short of breath as he spoke them.

"I—a-m—Y-a-n-k-e-l—S-c-h-m-u-l-o-w-i-c-z."

"Can you have gone by another name . . . long ago, I mean . . ."

No, it was madness to ask!

A rueful smile stole over the stranger.

"I—h-a-v-e—g-o-n-e—b-y—m-a-n-y— n-a-m-e-s."

Slow Note Due

"Did you once, for example, call yourself—" But here, with a fillip of the finger, Schmulowicz sealed up Gernsbacher's lips. Rabbi wished to say more but found he could not. Two red spots rose up on his wan cheeks.

"M-a-n-y—n-a-m-e-s.—Y-o-u—m-u-s-t—d-e-c-i-d-e."

Schmulowicz led rabbi to supper. As if snowblind, bedazed, he with difficulty took his seat. A ham and cheese sandwich was laid before him. Reader, he ate it.

CHAPTER FOURTEEN

Suitable Darkness

THIS FEAST of the inedible revived Gernsbacher, brought him round. He found he
could speak again. "Excuse me," he said and
stepped out back of the boathouse. He bent
over, hands on his knees, intending to relinquish
what he had eaten. But that sandwich sat comfort-
ably on rabbi's stomach; that sandwich wanted to
stay down.

He stood upright, wiped his pewter-colored face
with a kerchief, went back inside.

"Come along, young fellow," he said to Felix, "I
will be taking you back to town."

"Well, sir, I'm with him," Felix replied, indicating Wick.

"Yeah, he's with me. Anyhow, we're on our bikes."

More cheek from that one, that Esau.

"Felix may certainly put his bicycle in the back of my wagon," replied rabbi to Wick. "You are on your own, young man."

Now, as if in appeal to a higher court, the boys turned to Schmulowicz.

"G-o—a-l-o-n-g—F-e-l-i-x," the stranger urged.

Rabbi pulled his hat straight. "On your own," he reiterated to Wick.

"I myself don't need no lift anyhow, reverend," Wick answered, winking heavily at Felix and Schmulowicz. "Got me some work to do—summer job in the evenings and, well sorry, but I just ain't got time to be riding back in your old wagon. Be late if I did."

Then, in a whisper, brushing past Felix: "Meet me you-know-where at eleven."

Out the door Wick went and off on his bicycle, struggling down the sandy path, wobbling, sinking down, starting up manfully again.

Felix gathered up his belongings.

"A-n-d—w-o-n-t—y-o-u—b-e—w-a-n-t-i-n-g—t-h-i-s?" Schmulowicz held up the little unguent jar this way and that, then slipped it into the boy's shirt pocket. "F-o-r—w-h-a-t-e-v-e-r—a-i-l-s."

Felix's mother kept slipping his mind. He could not hold her there, conspire though the world might to remind him. Your mother, said the floor, the crossbeams, the doorjamb, the bayou and field of saw-edged grass beyond, the sun aflame this late afternoon in a hackberry tree.

"Your mother will be very happy to see you, I am certain," Gernsbacher said.

Seated beside rabbi in the buckboard, travelling silently back to town, Felix again thought of something else. His bicycle was wedged behind them, the handlebars sticking up. Onward they jolted.

"Tell me, sir, what does that cloud formation over there look like to you?"

Rabbi stirred from a brown study. What sort of foolishness was this, looking at clouds? "I haven't any idea," he answered.

"Close one eye and look again. You see? Looks just like President Roosevelt, giving a speech. That little part is the mustache, that square part is the forehead—see his outflung hand?"

Something lay ahead in the path, Gernsbacher saw. "What is it turning into now?" he asked Felix, and lashed the roan briskly.

"Into somebody else."

"Keep a close watch," rabbi said, his own eyes fastened to the road.

"Yes, turning . . . It's Mary, Queen of Scots. You see her? She's abdicating, conveying the crown to her son. She's naming the earl of Murray as regent."

Rabbi lashed the mare, and veered.

"Changing again," said Felix.

Gernsbacher wished to spare the boy what was there in the road. A long-tailed weasel lay dying, crushed across the haunches. Reddish and white, pencil thin, it gave a creaturely stare as the buckboard veered by.

"Top part's turning into—into—"

Now they were past, but not before Felix caught sight of the weasel. He swung round on the seat for a better look. "Still *alive*, did you see?"

"I did."

"So, stop!"

"We cannot help the unfortunate animal, my boy."

"We can put him out of his misery!"

"With what, with our bare hands? I haven't any gun. Do you imagine a rabbi goes on his errands with a gun?"

"Turn back, sir!"

In the mind's eye Gernsbacher saw himself strangling the last life out of the weasel; saw himself standing by while Felix did so. It would not do to turn back. Rabbi lashed the mare hard.

"You'd be too scared, wouldn't you? Turn back. *I'll* do it. With these," Felix said, holding up his hands. "I'm not scared." He folded his arms across his chest. "Of anything. Anymore."

With swimming eyes he turned for a last look, then hollered, "*I'M NOT SCARED!*" The strong cry rang away into woods and fields.

Rabbi urgently wanted to get this problem case back to town. It had been enough of a Sunday. He laid the switch to the mare, turned his eyes to the bayou, lying like amber beneath a late afternoon sun.

Suitable Darkness

Only now did he permit himself to think on what the stranger had unfolded. Causing his life, as they say, to pass before him. Who was this Yankel Schmulowicz, who knew him to his entrails? Try as he might, Gernsbacher could not bring to the test of thought what he had beheld on the tiny stage. Was it no more than what the gentiles called art, a trifling with idols? No, this was not art; this was *visitation*, Gernsbacher knew.

But by whom? Like water dashed in his face came an answer. Elijah the Tishbite, who never died. *Eliyahu ha giladi*, assumed bodily into heaven. He comes back to us. If life is a vale, Elijah is the thoroughfare cutting through. He is the road and the wayfarer upon it. And lo, farther on, the hard track up the mountain, that is Elijah too. Sometimes he is called names like supernatural, sublime. But these are names for what cannot be named—this abyss of humanness into which we reach, not knowing where the bottom lies.

Call him what you will. In the shadow, in the quiver, he waits. And is suddenly, expeditiously among us. He is timely. You do not seep back into earth before he finds you. He cuts a path across your own; then, by the change of his name, the turning of his cloak, becomes someone else. Drags down the road his body green with age. He does not die . . .

These should have been sacred thoughts, flesh-bound presentiments of eternity. But, no. Today rabbi saw Elijah for what he was, only another wandering disinheritance, cast out upon the high road no less than we. For Elijah, too, the way up the mountain leads back down to this deep trouble. Ah, there may or may not be Otherness. But Other is what it remains. For us there is only this flesh. This flesh which is mostly water. In other words, mostly tears.

How different that long-ago time when a Breslau book vendor had urged on Nathan the volume in green. Prologue, that had been. Later on, assailed by doubt, he would cut more pages and read another tale, thereby regaining faith; each time his purpose broke he'd read from the little book to mend it. And remember a feckless vow he'd sworn to wait for seventy. And now he *was* seventy, and the tales were all read, and the little green volume, carried from the Old World to the New, sat on the shelf and paid him no mind. To be left without a prayer, thus was he punished; to have come resourceless, empty-handed to this day.

After reading the last tale—how long ago was it? perhaps eight or ten years—he'd gone in fear and trembling; surely, he would die now. But the weeks lengthened out into months, the months into years, and here he still was, waiting for an end. As a child he had trusted to what his mother, of blessed memory, said—that speedily and in their time would come a conclusion of days, the portents of history fulfilled, the house of earth set in messianic order. This afternoon proclaimed something else: a world nowhither going, life only life forever more, a swift, swift arrow never gaining its mark. Gernsbacher's heart of wisdom pounded hard. He told himself—*This you must bear. A world unsponsored, unprophesiable. This you must bear.* And wondered was he Jewish anymore, thinking such thoughts.

A Jew could say: we are punished as surely as the weasel in the road. On Job's authority a Jew could say this. What you dared not do was take the next step. You dared not curse the Punisher. You could say this is a God who sometimes hides His face. You could say, in other words, that He is inscrutable. What you dared not say was that He is indifferent, too busy to see us there in our torments. For such a God would merit curses.

Asked just what this Lord does all day, one of the great rabbis (not a poor latter-day sort like Gernsbacher but a sage of the Talmudic times) answered that the Almighty sits down each morning in the justice seat and surveys His creation. And He is wroth with all He sees, and resolves to make a short work of it, lay waste this splendor. Imagine suns, planets, moons fired out, consumed in the instant, all fair things annihilated to nothingness.

But immediately God takes this decision, He goes and sits down in the mercy seat, beholds again His handiwork, resolves to wait another day. By this clemency we toil on, damned and reprieved and damned and reprieved and . . .

It was a pretty tale, improving for children. Perhaps he should narrate it to the truculent boy beside him. Drawing in a breath of country air, though, he found he hadn't the fortitude left to tell of God's diurnal decisions. Oh, Gernsbacher was *tired* of being a rabbi! The old high words were as sounding brass. Today a difference was overtaking him, a forbidden new knowledge declaring itself. God existed, to be sure. And was omnipotent— Almighty, as they say.

But not good.

Were He good, He'd have made a fitter world. Why ever this one, compact of loneliness and madness, disease and death? Was such His mercy? For such were we to praise Him? No more, no more. The convolved thinking of a lifetime—faith, doubt—gave way now to plain certainty, bankable as the grave: in this wilderness of a universe there is but one seat of mercy, and that is ourselves. Gernsbacher acceded forthwith to the wisdom of Job's wife. He cursed . . .

No earthquake, wind, or fire. Only the wide quietness, the lad beside him, the mare clomping equably onward. His interdicted thought kept him good company: we are all there is of mercy. Encouraged, he cursed again . . . Nothing. No signs.

Gernsbacher's was not the usual imprecation. *All praise to man* was what he said to himself, happy as the dry stick that puts forth a shoot. *All praise to man for his mercy*. A mental whisper, still and small, no miracle to it. Slowly, with due emphasis to each word, "*Far zayn rakhmones, geloybt zol zayn der mentsh,*" he said. The despised mother tongue was luminous and sure today, a jargon of angels.

Rabbi pulled the roan up short, handed the reins to Felix, leapt down, took her by the bit. She did as he wished, came round. Rabbi stroked her snout, gave her a handful of oats, climbed back up.

Felix understood. They were going back.

The weasel, when they got there, seemed to be waiting. No panic; composure; relief, perhaps. A heavy spittle hung from its mouth.

Felix went to the side of the road, to where some bunchgrass grew, and pulled up handfuls of it till he'd cleared a spot. He knelt down and dug a hole, piling up the sandy soil to either side.

Gernsbacher picked up a rock. He had never killed anything so large as this. The weasel stared. Rabbi used one hand to gather up the scruff of the neck. Then he brought down the sharp end of the rock in a glancing blow. The weasel writhed, stretched out in the dust. Rabbi held him firm and struck again, this time to good effect. The weasel died. Now rabbi took off his hat, placed the weasel inside, who fit snugly there. Holding it from underneath, he brought the hat to the grave Felix had dug. Felix spread his handkerchief over the hat, which rabbi then placed in the ground. Together they put the earth back into the hole, and patted the mound till it was firm. They brushed the sandy soil from their hands, remounted the buckboard and, with nothing to say, rode on to town.

Sleep cure," Neevah said, wanting to believe that Lucy would waken—herself again, restored—from that day's heavy drawn-out slumbers. Neevah spoke low as she went about her tasks. She heard the evening train sound its horn, highballing across the causeway, growing faint now, disappearing. The house filled up with shadows.

When rabbi brought Felix home earlier that afternoon Neevah had flatly refused to speak to the boy. He went to his room and opened *Aeneidos* by P. Vergilius Maro. Casting his eyeglasses aside, he read of two gates of sleep—the one of plain horn, through which true dreams straightly come; the other of glorious ivory, through which the false dreams issue. *Sunt gemini Somni portae.* Felix licked his pencil point and went to work. "Of the portals of sleep there are two . . ." he translated. After some reflection, he saw his way clear to the next part: ". . . one of horn, through which the true dreams pass with ease, the other of flawless polished ivory, and yet false dreams are sent by this way to the upper world." *His ibi tum natum Anchises prosequitur dictis portaque emittit eburna.* "And here Anchises took the Sibyl and his son together," Felix translated, "and urged them out by the ivory gate."

Ivory? Horn, surely. Had Virgil here nodded off? Or was this something to make you think again? Bloodline of Assaracus through Romulus flowing, Junius Brutus taking back the fasces, Camillus bearing the lost standards home, Torquatus with his axe, the Decii and the Drusi, Fabius delaying, great Cato, Julius and all the Ascanian line, Augustus ushering in a longed-for Age of Gold—false dreams, these? The poet sends the sibyl and the hero armed with images of Roman grandeur through—mark this now!—the lying *ivory* gate. A wink from P. Vergilius to F. Mehmel, across the eighty generations? Evidently so.

Suitable Darkness

Felix in triumph stretched out for a little nap.

When he waked up he heard the clock in the hallway ringing eleven. He sat upright, rubbed his eyeglasses with his shirttail, put them on. Felix had a purpose. He listened for sounds about the house; he went to the door, peeked out. All clear. He made his way downstairs and to the kitchen, then out the back door, careful not to bang the screen behind him. Though hungry, he thought it more prudent not to eat.

There Wick was when he arrived, against a stanchion supporting an arc-light, having himself a smoke. It was the corner of Market and Twenty first.

"You ready?" Felix asked.

Wick stamped out his cigarette in the dust, cast his eyes askance. He looked shifty at this late hour, bloodshot. "Got something to show you," he said.

His summer work was to clean regularly at several offices around town—mopping hallways, washing windowsills, carrying off waste paper, and so forth. Wick liked these evening jobs. He felt free to work at his own pace, knocking off from time to time to see what might be under the unlocked roll-top of a desk or in a filing cabinet or on the top shelf of a closet. Interesting things came to light.

Wick wasn't larcenous, only nosy. After inspecting things he put them back how they were. Of particular interest this week was the cache of bitterly reproachful love letters to a senior partner of Fordyce, Meekens, Heaviside & Carew, Attorneys at Law, from a woman not that senior partner's wife. Wick hooted and hollered and whistled low as he read them.

On Market and Twenty-first, one flight up from Fordyce, Meekens *et al*, was the office of old Dr. Loren Bidwell, family physician, dried-up Yankee. Wick liked looking up the names of persons he knew in Bidwell's files. Unlike most of the doctors whose offices Wick cleaned, Bidwell wrote an excellently legible hand. It was an education to examine the many things he'd noted down over the years. Wick read of lumbago and of gout, of breakbone fever, blood poison, scarlatina, fast heart disease, diphtheria, infantile paralysis, ulcer, impetigo, ringworm, carbuncle, whelk, and bunion. He read of cloven palate and softening of the brain, of milk leg and bloody flux. What a world! What a *world* in which you could catch such things!

"Come on up to Bidwell's," said Wick to Felix.

When they got there, Wick went to the file cabinet, leafed through to the letter M, pulled out the yellowed record of "Mehmel, Aharon." "This here was your old man, right?"

Felix made no answer.

"Looky." Wick pointed to a word underscored twice in the file. "You know what that means? Cupid's itch. Your daddy had him a case of it." Wick reached for *Merck's Manual of the Materia Medica*, there on Bidwell's desk, and opened it to the appropriate entry. There was a photograph of a sad-faced naked man, his body covered with lumpish spots. "Lookahere . . ."

And Felix took a long, long look, feeling as if launched upon a dangerous sea . . .

It occurred to him that the dead hadn't any right to secrets. They should tell their stories without expurgation and tell them now. He could recollect, confusedly, the sight of his father breaking down once, speaking German through tears. Felix had been sent immediately from the room. No, the dead had no right to secrets.

"Lookahere—'congenially transmitted.' You know what that means, don't you? Children gets it from their parents."

Now a little smile budded onto Felix's lips. "If you say so, Wick."

"Means someday you'll look like this." And he pointed to the man with the spots.

Oh, why do we put up with these brutes? Don't ask. It has to do with our wish to know what it would be like to be like them, to wear the comely frown, see the world with setter eyes. But hasn't it to do finally with some obscurer wish—to make *them* wonder what it would be like to be like *us*? Forget it; they are not the wondering kind.

"Someday will see to itself," Felix told him. "What I'm strictly interested in is tonight. You're ready for what we planned, aren't you?"

Wick pulled his mouth to one side, gave a shrug.

"Oh, no, Mr. Wick Frawley, you're not ducking out on me, not here at the last minute."

"I—well, I think, you know, we ought to think it over."

Suitable Darkness

"Turn around, please. Turn around. And no peeking."

Now Felix took the unguent jar out of his pocket. He put it on Bidwell's desk, and began peeling off his clothes—the shirt first, then the shoes, the knickers and stockings, till he stood quite naked. He opened the jar and set about smearing himself. Felix worked the salve into the tops of his feet, the soles too; his back and front, not forgetting the navel; now behind the knees; now some for his face, his hair. Felix put his clothes back on, returned the jar to his pocket.

"You may turn around now."

Wick turned, said: "I don't think this is such a good idea anymore."

"Tell you what, Wick Frawley, you let me do the thinking. Simpler that way. You just go find us a cold chisel and a hacksaw. Steal them if you have to. Also a pine-knot, and some kerosene. I'll meet you in an hour out at the old barn." Felix took off his eyeglasses, blew a little on either lens, wiped them authoritatively on his shirt. "You be there," he wound up, putting the spectacles back on.

"Oh, and Wick," he added, as back outside they

took their leave of each other, "when you hit an animal in the road, one of two things is right to do. You nurse it, or you kill it. You don't leave it to suffer to death. I'll see you in one hour, Wick."

When Felix rode up, Wick was waiting as ordered. He had on him a cold chisel and a hacksaw. He'd lighted the pine-knot and was holding it aloft. The night had turned clammy on them. A fog like batting rose up from the ground and hid the moon. Felix took up the chisel. "Hold the torch this way," he ordered. He tried but failed to prize off the lock. He took up the hacksaw. Slow work. He tried the chisel, but feared the sound of his pounding might be heard. He went back to the hacksaw. Slow work, slow sawing . . .

Now the lock gave way, the doors opened. Snatching the pine-knot from Wick, Felix went in. He walked a circle around the glider. She looked jaunty in the firelight. "We'll take her out now."

Roache and Munger that afternoon had left the guy lines fastened on. Felix was surprised when he tugged at one to find how light the craft was. "Out of my way!" he told Wick, handing him the torch—

and grabbed up both lines, one over each shoulder, and pulled like a dray horse.

"Let's think this whole thing over," Wick begged. "I'm—"

The last word being too low for Felix to hear, "Come again," he said.

"—scared," Wick repeated. As if by way of proof, he'd started a nosebleed. Felix came up and very slowly, very gently took hold of Wick by the shirt front. "Where the hell's your self-respect?" he asked, pushing him backwards a little. "When I tell you, you put these lines over your shoulders and you run with this thing. You understand?"

Wick nodded.

"And wipe your nose."

Wick nodded.

Felix removed his eyeglasses and climbed in. A flame feebly clinging to Wick's pine-knot now extinguished itself in the sticky breeze. A suitable darkness supervened. He let the torch fall.

"Pull! *Pull! PULL!*" Felix bellowed in a piercing martial voice. And hell for leather Wick pulled, running down the rise. The fearless voice let out a *WHOOP!* . . . Wick crouched down, felt the backwash as Felix sheared over him. A long moment later came the thwack and slow noise of splitting asunder. The world shook for a moment and was still. Across the utter night a chirring of crickets ceased, resumed. Wick called out for Felix. Silence. He called again. No answer. The darkness poured into Wick's mouth. He swallowed and swallowed and the darkness poured in. Now he began to fight a path through the saw-edged grass, back to where he thought the road lay.

CHAPTER FIFTEEN

Causes of Things

UT THE HOT DARK DEPRIVED HIM of his bearings, and his search for the road led only in a futile circle. When it was clear to Wick that he'd got himself completely lost, he lay down in the wet grass; cried bitterly, noisily; then slept.

At the alarum of day Leo found him there, clothes torn by stickers and brambles, a crusted patch of blood smearing the upper lip. Leo had come out before dawn on a watch for bitterns. This being Labor Day, Galveston was sleeping in. Leo'd seen no one on his way to Offatts. He bent down now, gave the boy a shake.

Wick started up, sleep-drunk, not knowing where he was, raising a hand to fend off the daylight. He had a blessed moment of feeling only prickly in the grass, not remembering what had happened. Then the previous night flooded back, broke on him in a wave. He got giddily to his feet. The field spun round him once. On his cheeks a flush rose up. He staggered, hollow-kneed; was wrung and wrung; brought up a little bile.

Now he regained himself, reached out, dirty-faced, pulled Leo by the sleeve, urging him in the direction of the old barn. "Flying machine . . ."

"Yes?"

"Somebody's hurt."

Dropping his field glasses and bird ledger, fearing to know what was at the other end of Thigpen's, Leo pursued to the hangar, Wick cringing along behind him.

Now Leo ran. "It ain't my fault, you know!" Wick called out, unheard. Leo's arms threshed the air. Leo raced to the brow of the hill. Below, what did he see?

Debris, spread out in a moon shape. Flung a little ways off, the mound of clothes, flesh, bone. Wick cast a watery calflike eye to there, looked away, looked again.

On a nearer view, Leo knew the mound for Felix. He got down on his knees, laid an ear to the boy's chest, gathered him up and made for town.

The last of the Mehmels, there they went.

Wick followed, letting out now and then a desultory cry, reiterating how this was none of his fault.

In an uncle's arms, Felix dreamed a dream. He stood at the bottom of a narrow pit, looking upwards for a glimpse of sky. Miss Murph in a gingham shirtwaist was down there too. She turned on him her scratched-quartz eyes. Now, from behind his ear, she pulled the bough of gold. *I am dreaming*, Felix tried to tell himself. Ordinarily, you have only to say this to know it is true. But here, as if the power by which to distinguish between dreaming and waking had ceased to work, Felix could not persuade himself. *Very well*, he declared, *if I wake or I sleep!*

Fear had folded its tents, stolen away. Seeing this was so, Murph raised up the glittering tendril in her fist and showed him, by a hidden cleft of rock, the way . . . You know how dreams are. The scene changes. You are in one place, then another, without transition. But along the steep path of this dream were no such divides. Moment followed moment in a seamless clarity. It was the noontide of waking. Thus they passed down to the unlit world, the dark beneath the deep. Murph flung herself on, taller now, disarranged. *Stick to me like a bur, child!* she commanded. Felix felt for the footholds as he followed.

At the absolute bottom, to which they came, grows a tree each leaf of which is a blighted wish. Around this tree the wind goes in a circle, rampageous. New leaves appear as old ones fly off. The great-rooted bole—though sick at its core—will flourish forever, and utter no end of our failing. Behold, hard by, a bowed-down figure, hugging to him his cloak. Felix took a look, knew the crumpled shape—and knowing it knew now for a certainty the livelong endurance of those dead as of us living. Felix turned to Murph, but she was gone.

I am that father you lack! the bowed-down figure called out. Seeing the smile of pain on his face, Felix undertook to go to him, but kept losing the ground from under his feet. The shape undid his cloak, which the wind whipped up behind him. He showed his ravaged spotted self to Felix. He showed what life can do.

Now Felix managed the arduous struggle to his father. The bent shape released his cloak to the winds, grappled Felix to him, whispered,

Do not dream of another way. The wind went around in a circle, and carried off the leaves. *This is our necessity.* The wind went around in a circle. *After love comes grief,* said the bowed-down shape. The wind tore round and round. *And now, my life, you must go back.*

And that is what Felix did.

From his doorstep Schmulowicz saw them come up the towpath—Leo with the boy in arms, Wick following. Schmulowicz went forth. Like air he passed alongside of them, so they could not see. His work here was done. He took a last satisfied look at the boy in Leo's grasp and hastened back to his confine.

At the doorstep of the boathouse Schmulowicz now made a gesture, a slow whirl of the hand above his head. And a brace of crows, oily bright, came down to feed him bread and meat he washed down with water from the well.

He entered the house with one thing more to do. He ranged his puppets in a row, stepped back to admire them. And laughing aloud on his bare breath, he left them there, partly for a benediction, partly for a haunting. In vacant attitudes they watched him go.

Schumulowicz went now to the adjoining shed and reached up to where the old pirogue lay across the beams. He pulled on a grab-rope tied to the bow; down she came. A paddle clattered to the floor. He picked it up, stuck the narrow end into his string belt. In a motion, grabbing the vessel by the gunwales, he turned her keel-up, lowered her onto his shoulders. It was pleasantly dark under there. Schmulowicz tried out his unheard voice for the echo. It came feebly at first, singsong, like a windlass creaking; then clearer, stronger.

Words cannot say how marvelously he sang, and sings, whose portage now is to the ocean side. He carries the inverted pirogue to there, his song clamoring in the ribs of the hull. Elijah sings, earth lasts. He arrives at the wet edge, puts down his burden. A breeze fans his ancient cheek. He sniffs with pleasure the rank air. His paddle in one hand, he turns for a last look at cloud-set Galvez, mysterious in a morning fog. He walks his vessel out from the shelving shore. He turns to look again. See the shine of those old eyes! He settles himself on the stern thwart; dips his paddle; pulls hard for the open sea.

Concussed to the head, ripped open across an eye, his arm broken in two places, Felix Mehmel was slow to mend.

A little before dawn of that Labor Day Murph and Truley had received a telephone call from Neevah, who begged their pardon for the earliness of the hour but wanted to know did Felix spend the night with them, for his bed was empty. Neglecting even to take the papers from their hair, Murph and Truley rushed into the street, crying, "Felix! Felix!" —their housecoats flapping about them as they ran. Lights went on in one house after another of Winnie Street as folks climbed out of bed to see what the matter was.

The ladies spread out, Murph turning onto Eighteenth, Truley heading west along Post Office. Now came Leo up Winnie, Felix in arms, Wick tagging along still. When Murph saw them at the other end of the block, she put two fingers in her mouth and let out a splitting whistle. Three streets away Truley heard and came running. Murph reached them and received the boy into her arms. Now Truley caught up.

When they got back to the house Bob was tearing around the yard. He knew something bad had happened. Seeing them, he threw himself headlong at Truley's feet. "Not now, Bobby," she scolded in a low tone.

"Get Dr. Bidwell on the telephone," Murph said over her shoulder as she carried Felix up the stairs. She brought him into the sitting room, laid him on the divan, then went to the kitchen to prepare a compress. She found Wick in front of the open pantry, looking for something to eat.

"Lady, I'm hungry—been out there all night and—"

"I ought to run you off like a varmint," was all of her answer as she broke up ice in the sink and wrapped it in a washcloth. But she left Wick to forage as he pleased.

"Fast asleep, breathing regular," Truley told Dr. Bidwell over the telephone. "His color's tolerable. It's the eye and arm we're worried about." Bidwell said he would be there directly he could grab his bag.

Truley phoned Neevah, who'd returned home after wandering the streets herself in search of the boy. Truley asked her wouldn't she like to come see Felix but Neevah said no, Miss Lucy needed her, should not be alone.

Bidwell showed up without his necktie, the way a doctor should in an emergency. He hung his hat on the clothes tree in the front hall. Truley showed him up the stairs. First thing he did was to raise Felix's uninjured eyelid. The ladies stood together near the window. "You're in my light," he told them, bluntly Yankee. They moved to opposite corners. Bidwell now inspected the other eye, the hurt one. Lashed across the cornea; a nasty cut on the upper lid. Beginning to come to, Felix drew back in pain from the doctor's touch. Bidwell covered the good eye, asked, "Can you see me, son?"

"Some of you."

Bidwell washed the lid and applied an antiseptic bandage. He warned Felix that this would be itchy but that he musn't scratch, mustn't attempt even to open his eye beneath the bandage. Drifting in and out, Felix may or may not not have heard.

Now to the arm, a more difficult matter. "I'll need assistance from you ladies," said the doctor. He instructed Murph to take hold of the boy's shoulders and Truley of his feet. "Because he'll writhe, I expect." And writhe he did, coming fully to with a howl when Bidwell realigned the arm. "Hold him! Hold him!" Bidwell applied splints; wrapped Felix from the wrist to the shoulder; told him, over the boy's pleadings—for he was now fully awake, and in agony—to get some rest.

A racket accompanied by savory smells was coming up the backstairs from the kitchen. Without so much as by your leave, Wick Frawley had commenced to fry eggs and bacon.

It had been a disappointing Labor Day, all would afterwards agree. Two hundred or more of the town, convening at noon to watch Roache and

Munger's flying exhibition, were left to gawk at the vacant air. Purvis, Jr. galloped up on horseback to inform them that such things as flying were dangerous and wouldn't be permitted. "Everybody get on home!" he scolded. All tempers were spoiled. Purvis told the crowd they could read in next day's papers, if they chose, about a young boy practically killed the night previous through this mischief of wanting to fly.

When old man Fewtrell learned of Felix Mehmel's near brush he told Roache and Munger that if they valued their jobs they wouldn't undertake construction of another such infernal device. But Roache and Munger stood right up to Fewtrell. They told him he had better find two other mechanics, for Galveston had palled on them. They would move north, they told him—to Lufkin, or maybe Nacogdoches. Fewtrell rang the register and handed them their severance and didn't even care to shake hands.

The weeks passed by, the days drew in. A Mrs. Clarence Spingarn came to town on the train. She wore a hat in the shape of a bucket and, pinned to the hat, a heavy brooch. She carried her own suit-

case, declining all assistance, drawing the attention of people as she labored along Broadway, for Mrs. Spingarn was of a vastness. Townsfolk stared all but frankly at this traveler, the view of whom from the rear put them in mind (several of the ungentlemanly class were quick to note) of hogs fighting under a wagon sheet.

Mrs. Spingarn presently found the house, mounted the front steps, rang the bell. Neevah opened the door, stared dully. Now her eyes widened. She put a callused palm to the fat lady's cheek. "It's you, baby, ain't it?"

"It's me, Neevah."

Neevah didn't know what to say; she only said what came to mind. "Is you the same, or different?"

"The same," Molly said.

And Neevah folded her close. "Fine old married lady, that's what you is!"

Neevah reared back for another look, clutching Molly by the arms. "Honey, I done clean forgot what you call your married self. Some funny name.

"Spingarn."

"Thas right. You come right on in this house, Miz Spingarn . . . while it's still ours."

Molly did not admire the marvels of the place—the newel post supporting a crystal globe, the pier mirrors in their gilt frames, the genuine Chinese urn in a niche. Nor did she notice that on each exquisite object of the foyer a little tag had been hung. "Neevah, take me to her," was what she said.

But Neevah wished her not to go upstairs unprepared. "Miss Lucy, she know she's confused. Sometimes she don't see I'm looking, and she rub her hands together like she done got through something, like she out of her trouble. Then her trouble come back on her. Mind you, she is *sweet* all the time treats everybody the same. She starts patting you, and she says, 'I'm happy, *so* happy to see you.' But she don't never call nobody by they name. Thas how you know she ain't right in her mind. Oh, but sweet, Miss Molly, *sweet!* I done found her one day in the attic, going through clothes. What do you think she pulled out? Little old dress of hers, something from even before she was married. White turnover collar, pearl buttons. She said, 'I'll wear this.' I said,

honey, that don't suit you no more. She didn't care none. She went and *got* herself into that dress, old yellow terrible-looking thing. And what do you think, ever since—I can't get her out of it. Yestidday I was doing my best to talk to, well, I guess you'd call him a second-hand man the bank done sent over here. White respeckful gentleman. Sorry, he said, about what he was doing. Had a sad job, he told me, having to put these here tags on all the—what'd he call them? Con-vert-i-ble assets. And here comes Miss Lucy down the stairs with a *big* hello for him, you'd think he was a friend. Now don't be upset when you see her hair. Growing out slow. Mistah Aharon's momma, she come over here sometimes, not too often. Because she say one loonatic to look after is enough. Lawd, thas why it all done fell out on me. You think Neevah get herself a rest at the end of the day? Neevah be running like a scalded dog." At the landing of the stairs she stopped, considered. "Loonatic ain't no word for it, not for what Miss Lucy got." And she led Molly down the hall to the room where by herself Lucy sat. Vastly forgetful, empty-eyed in a wingback chair, "Happy to see

you! Happy, happy to see you!" she cried. The eyes shone. A fathomless smile stole onto her lips, lingered out. Lucy had left them behind, Molly saw now, the way dreams get left. Forgotten at the sundering of sleep. Lucy lived at a distance, the oblivion a winding sheet marvelously about her.

"I'll take you home, sugar. To Newawlens. That's where you'll get better. You and your little boy can live with us. My Clarence, that *saint* of a man, said to me, 'You got kinfolk in a bad way, Molly, you bring them on back here.'" Brightening, seeking for the note of life as it ought to be, Molly grew flustered despite herself. A helplessness said in her throat: "Where's Felix? Where *is* that child? Time for me to set eyes on him!"

"Gone from here. Staying over to them two ladies' house, on Winnie."

"Staying, Neevah?"

"Over on Winnie, with them ladies of his."

"By staying, you mean living?"

"Thas right."

"I do not understand. The boy's not of an age to leave home. The boy is, what—fifteen?"

"Fixing to be."
"I certainly do not understand."
"It ain't no home left here."

The harvest was past, the summer was ended, they were not saved. Leo gave up his rooms at Tremont House. Confronting fundamentals, he returned to the residence of his parents at Sealy and Sixteenth. The corner bedroom where he'd grown up was again his narrow cell. Visible in an attic dormer of the house was something new—the considerable telescope which after many sulks he had prevailed upon his mother to buy for him. Queer restless fellow, he'd given up ornithology, was all out now for stargazing.

On a certain house of limestone and blue granite, one block north and four west of there, the mortgage was at the end of that October to be foreclosed. Quietus, final settlement. Felix Mehmel had walked out the door, home had dissolved behind him. No, Molly didn't try now to persuade the boy to New Orleans with them. Neevah told her not to. She knew (having seen it before) the unassailable look of one who has left home. In Felix's unbandaged eye, where a tear should have been, stood the snowy Apennines.

Old Orvis Truley, inveterate half-wit of the town, who'd slunk along the margins of Lucy's widowed life and loved her fiercely from that distance, stepped forth now, bowed deep, asked if he mightn't have the honor of conveying the widow Mehmel's luggage to the depot. Hildy poked her head up out of Lucy's draw-string bag; inspected this man Aharon Mehmel had saved at the expense of his own life; rolled upwards and shut her heavy topaz eyes. Molly watched as Orvis gathered their suitcases—one in each hand, one under each arm. Hildy ducked back down into Lucy's reticule. Without stopping to rest, Orvis carried their baggage all the way to the station, Molly and Lucy and Neevah coming along after him. When they got to the platform Molly offered him ten cents for his trouble. He shook his head no.

"If you aren't," she exclaimed, "an angel on the face of the earth! *Take* this dime, mister!"

Now Orvis turned to Lucy and, swift about it, helped himself to a kiss, for that and not ten cents was what he wanted.

Molly raised her umbrella. "Miserable, *nasty!*"

And "You get on out of here!" Neevah bellowed as to a cur dog. She took out her handkerchief, wiped Lucy's mouth.

The sun shone broad there, the waste light spilled down. From up where clouds were packing, from up where heaven was, Galveston must only have looked like a ridge of marl. Or like a floating spar, flotsam of some wrack. But what is essential to say is that this place existed, that these people existed, and were in one another's keeping, and stood still in the lee of an instant—even if they and their island should forever slip the mind of God, mattering no more to Him than a thirsty handful of earth flung up at the sky. The heavier pieces come straight down, but the fine ghost hangs awhile, moving sidewise, and settles onto your upturned face.

Secret is: to know from outcomes the long way back. Happy the man who's learned causes of things. Happy despite the patch on the eye, the splints on the arm. Reading now as for dear life, he comes upon this: *Felix qui potuit rerum cognoscere cau-*

Causes of Things

sas. Homage from P. Vergilius to F. Mehmel, across the chasm of centuries? Evidently so. He takes up his pen, writes: "Felix is the man who learns causes of things!" And turns out his bed lamp, lies waiting for sleep.

From the back yard comes a sound of connubial murmurs, and of water being poured. The osage drops its heavy fruit. The island sighs. In a galvanized tub, by the guide of the moon, Murph is washing Truley.